THE HIGH SCHOOL QUEENS TRILOGY BOOK TWO

THE REVENGED QUEEN

REVENGE IS BEST SERVED AS YOU KISS THEM ON THE LIPS AND STAB THEM IN THE HEART.

Gary,
I hope you're ready for round two.

ZACHARY RYAN

Copyright

Table of Contents

Chapter 1

The Marked Queen; you became our idol after the spectacular show you displayed at prom. Taking the throne can be an easy task, but keeping it from other bitches was where the true fun came into play. Bethany, why do you look so scared by a simple text? Are you going to let The Revenged Queen get under your skin so quickly? We were a bit ashamed, we thought you would take the Danielle Tyler approach. Well, she was your bitch, and you still exposed her truths. Were your skeletons going to stay in the closet or were they going to be exposed in the same fashion? What better way to send the seniors off than with a royal showdown at graduation?

"Baby, are you okay?" Tucker asked, looking at her.

Bethany smiled. "Yes, I'm perfectly fine." She put her phone in her bag. She would deal with this new threat another time. Do you really think that was wise? Bethany, we should give you a quick tip about being the newly found queen; never let a bitch have time to plan an attack. Bethany, Jasmine, Carter, Aman, Andrew, and Delilah gave you too much time, and we all saw how prom ended.

"I just hope people don't hate us," Susan said.

Susan, why didn't you just go sing to the birds at this point? No one cares if you feel guilty for exposing people's secrets.

"We did what we needed to do to get ahead in this school. Everyone needed to learn what they did, and I'm not going to let anyone make us the enemy. They did it to themselves." Bethany turned to Susan. "Besides, we made Jasmine run to Europe because she couldn't deal with the fact that no one liked her abused, fat ass."

Susan wanted to open her mouth, but she learned from Jasmine to keep her mouth shut. "I better get to History class. I'll see you all later."

"Do you think she's going to crack?" Tucker asked.

Bethany shrugged. "She needs to learn that we have no one to fear." Bethany saw Danielle trying to talk to Delilah. "I need to go." She leaned forward and gave Tucker a chaste kiss.

"Don't start drama. I thought we were above it all."

Bethany turned to look at him. "That was before I was revealed to be The Marked Queen." Bethany winked and began walking toward Danielle and Delilah.

"I want nothing to do with you. I have to meet with the fucking board of education because of you. Fuck you, Danielle," Delilah yelled. She wanted Danielle to leave her alone. She had enough problems on her plate, and the worst was the disappointment from Mr. Rozengota.

Danielle felt defeated, but she wasn't going to give up on Delilah that quickly. Bethany walked right up next to her. "Is there trouble in paradise?"

Danielle turned to see Bethany. "Don't you have a nerd to blow?"

Bethany laughed. "Please, you think your little insults are going to hurt my feelings." She touched her pearls. "I don't let the poor bruise my ego."

Danielle crossed her arms and smiled. "You really let this new-found fame get to your head. I must say that you're doing a good job of being humble." She turned to see Susan being scared at her locker. "It looks like one of your minions is about to pee her pants."

Bethany tuned and groaned at Susan. "She'll learn to get it together."

Danielle clapped her hands. "I can't wait to see how well that turns out. She did backstab Jasmine after all."

"You would know everything about backstabbing people, wouldn't you?"

Danielle sized her up. She didn't have time to deal with Bethany's bullshit. She was trying to fix things with Delilah, and it was becoming increasingly problematic. She saw Aman with his new girlfriend, and Aman's stares toward Calvin, who was trying to ignore him. She looked over to see Emily at her locker trying to ignore all the stares she was getting from people. "You made a lot of enemies from that little stunt you pulled."

"Are you saying you didn't make enemies when you were queen?"

"I didn't open the flood gates for people to expose other's secrets the way you did. You made this game way more interesting, if you ask me."

"How so?"

Danielle laughed. "Because now people are going to find what you got lurking under your bed. Bethany, you act like you're the one with nothing to hide, but that makes me believe you have the most to lose. I've got nothing else to hide, but you do. This is the first time it's best to show all your cards," Danielle said. Danielle was right. You made a foolish error, and you were going to be paying for it sooner or later.

"While you think that I should fear people, I want you to remember that I was the one that changed the rules. I'm invincible."

"And that's what's going to make it so much more divine when someone takes you down."

Bethany thought about The Revenged Queen in that moment. "Are you saying you're going to be coming after me now?"

Danielle shook her head. "Why would I take that satisfaction from another girl? You made one hell of a bed of knives. I hope you can sleep comfortably in it." She walked past Bethany leaving her with that moment of thought.

Bethany turned to see Danielle go up to Calvin, but Bethany she was loyal. She didn't backstab any of her friends, and that was how she would survive all of this. There was just weeks until graduation. It took her months to take down a kingdom. She doubted people would take her down so easily.

She felt her phone go off. She saw it was from the same number.

Unknown Number: *What? You didn't believe my declaration to you the first time? That's fine, The Marked Queen. I don't mind beheading you. You'll look less bloated.*

Bethany, you caused a lot of drama, and you were going to need to live with the consequences. We hoped you loved your moment of fame, because we thought your fall from grace was going to come way quicker than you thought. Bethany looked around, trying to find out who was sending the texts.

Jordan looked from afar as she closed her phone. She laughed, knowing that Bethany seemed bothered. She was disappointed in Danielle for not stopping this bitch sooner, but she had no problem doing it herself. Did the slut queen finally take the cock out of her mouth to reimagine herself? We guess fucking both the football team and lacrosse team was too much of a bore. Why not enter the ring as the new villain? What a that your mouth might be full of warts, but we heard you were talented.

Val, Jordan's sister, walked into the room as Brad was leaving. "You know you're supposed to please them before they run off," she said. Val had a petite frame, long brown hair, blue eyes, and she had a thing for lollipops. We wonder where these Caraway girls got their oral fixation from.

Jordan looked at her sister. She was happy she was home from college, but she didn't need her shit right now. "Don't you have a frat party to go to?"

Val laughed. "I'm leaving in a little bit, young sprout." She walked over and sat down next to her. "You're really going to let this bitch get to you? What I heard is that she is just some wallflower at your school."

Jordan turned to her sister. "She ruined everyone's lives."

"Or, you all were cowards, and you let your secrets get the best of you."

"Are you saying you don't have secrets?" Jordan asked.

Val twirled her lollipop. "Please, we all have some skeletons. What I'm telling you is that you all were stupid to let her use your secrets against you." She paused. "Or maybe she gave you the best revenge."

"How so?"

"Jordan, do I need to teach you everything?" She stood up. "Use that bitch's secrets against her."

"She's a fucking nerd. The only secret she probably has is that her pearls are fake."

Jordan, we could help you find some dirt on her for you. We heard she had an urgent email she quickly buried. We were still wondering what that was all about. You might want to check into that for us.

Chapter 4

"I can't do this," he said to Jordan.

Jordan looked at the guy she was trying to sleep with. Since The Marked Queen announced she was a whore, none of the guys at her school wanted to sleep with her. Aw Jordan, it was okay. We knew that you didn't have any diseases, but none of the boys knew that.

"Really, Brad? Why not?"

Brad got up. He still had an erection in his tight, black boxer briefs. We had to admit, Jordan had great taste in her playthings. "It was fun for a while, but people talk." He threw his phone on the bed. "What if people found out we had sex?"

She grabbed his phone and saw an article in a local gossip magazine about Jordan's many night lovers. "This fucking wuss." She thought it would stick to Johnson Prep, but it got out to the whole Upper East Side. "It means nothing, Brad."

"I have a reputation to keep."

She rolled her eyes. "Oh please, we know you aren't a virgin or loyal to that bitch of a girlfriend." Jordan got up. She ran her fingers down his torso toward his manhood. She grabbed him by the balls. "Don't be such a bitch," she said. Jordan was a happy girl until someone took her pleasure away from her.

He shuttered for a minute. "I can't do this. I'm sorry. I can't be labeled one of your victims." He grabbed her hand, and he gently pulled her hand off of his balls. He grabbed his clothes like the coward he was. "Maybe when things cool down, we can start back up." He gave her a weak smile as he left.

Jordan, we thought Jasmine was the one that scared the boys away. You must work on those blow jobs of yours. We get just want to say we are proud she was turning into a boring, do gooder.

"You've ruined our daughter, and she'll be crawling right back to me." He grabbed the credit card and walked toward the door. "You're going to regret this, Danielle, and I'll make it even harder to get this all back." He opened the door and slammed it shut.

Lily and Danielle kept calm for a moment. Lily walked over and gave her daughter a gentle squeeze. "I don't want you to ever regret that." We felt like she would when she found out the bomb you were keeping from her. Will that moral high ground be worth it then?

"I just don't want to be that evil person anymore." Danielle still laid awake at night burning with regret for destroying her friendship with Delilah.

"You'll fix all the mistakes that you've made. You have to be faithful." Lily kissed her on the cheek. "I need to get to work." She grabbed her apron off the kitchen table. When she did, papers fell off the table onto the floor.

"Let me get those," Danielle said. She leaned down to see an eviction notice on the ground. "Mom, what is this?" Danielle asked.

Lily smiled. "It's fine. We will make it up. I thought we were doing okay financially, but I was wrong. I guess I'm still trying to get ahold of paying bills on time."

Aw Danielle, you really were going to be a peasant. Well, most peasants had homes to live in. Maybe you shouldn't have told your dad to shove it now. We told you that the spoiled Danielle was the best version of you, or at least she had a house to live in.

Zachary Ryan

"Mom, we could have used dad's help. I could have still gone to the charity events with him."

Lily shook his head. "We will do this on our own."

"Mom, don't let your pride get to you," Danielle said.

"No, I won't go back to that man. I'm a strong woman, and I'll figure this out." She grabbed her keys. "I'll pick up shifts at work. You don't need to worry about it," Lily said. She walked toward the door holding her tears back.

Danielle crossed her arms. "I hope your pride keeps us warm at night on the streets."

Lily turned to her daughter. "You don't get to attack me. I'm not the one that lost their way."

"Please, you still haven't figured out how to be on your own." She paused. "Let's see what the great Lily can do now."

Lily didn't say anything. She opened the door and left for work. She knew her daughter was right. She was still the spoiled housewife, and she had no clue what she was going to do now. She was about to lose everything due to her pride. She spent the train ride to work wondering if she should call Ethan and suck it up.

Danielle rolled her eyes. She was disappointed in her mother, but she shouldn't have been surprised. Her mother wasn't the strongest person, even if she tried to put on a mask. She pulled out her phone, and she called the one person she could think of.

"I thought I would never see your number pop up on my phone," he said.

Danielle rolled her eyes. "Christian, I need help from you."

"Mysterious."

"Just meet me at The Rosewood tomorrow at 7." She hung up before he could reply. What do you have planned under

14

your sleeve, Danielle? We were wondering how this bitch was going to handle poor chic. Danielle, we didn't want you finding yourself another sugar daddy. You already have Dan. Oh wait... We told you numerous times to get rid of the poor stable boy. Are you finally going to suck cock for money? Christian wouldn't be bad as the first client. Desperate measures for a desperate wannabe.

Chapter 3

"You slept with a principal." Erika looked at Delilah with such disdain. They had just had their meeting with the board of education. Erika leaned over and grabbed herself a scotch.

Delilah looked out the limo window. She knew her mother was pissed, and she had to look at Principle Grand as he denied the allegations. "It wasn't true."

"Bullshit," Erika said, taking a sip of her drink. "I saw how much it hurt you that he said those things about you. I knew there was something going on between you two. We all could see it."

Delilah looked at her mother. "Then why did they just tell me I needed to take after school lessons? Why not expel me?"

"The reputation of Johnson Prep is too important to them. Plus, there was no proof." She looked out the window. "Is this why you cut yourself? Did you think so poorly of yourself?"

Delilah looked down at her fingers. "I told you that I was going through a lot of emotions the past couple of months."

"You're a writer. You should have poured it out on paper, not gotten on your knees for an older man," Erika said.

Come on, Erika. We all knew this was far better than her getting her feelings out. You weren't there for The Marked Queen's entrance, and we had to tell you it wouldn't have been as glorious without Danielle backstabbing Delilah.

Delilah laughed. "You think everything is quickly solved with a pen and paper."

Erika placed her glass down. "Well, if you kept your legs closed then we wouldn't have a scandal on our hands. I think there are benefits to a pen and paper."

Delilah rolled her eyes. "You didn't think I was good enough until a couple of weeks ago. You can't hold this against me."

"You were fucking your principle."

"And it would have stayed hidden if it wasn't for Danielle," Delilah said.

Delilah, we hoped you didn't forget the bitch that ruined your life. Now, we suggest you sleep with Dan, but you might still be scarred from the last nerd you tried to fall for.

"It's not her fault," Erika said. "They're poor, and we should be sympathetic to them."

"Please, she's a fucking bitch, and she knew what she was doing. She was trying to protect herself."

"Maybe you should have done the same damn thing," Erika looked at her daughter. She had no clue how they went array with her. She thought she and Matt did a good job of raising her. But weren't you trying to push her away from writing, and isn't Matt not really in the picture? It must suck thinking you were an excellent parent, and the proof tells otherwise.

Delilah looked out the window. She closed her eyes and took in a deep breath. She wanted to forget everything about prom, but she couldn't. She saw the sheer amusement from all of her classmates. She now had everyone thinking she was a giant whore. "I could never be so cruel."

Delilah, stop being a pathetic girl. We wanted you to be a bitch now. We get that you got used to being the slut, but those days are behind you. You pushed both the men that were using you out of the way. There would be no love in your life, so why not focus on revenge? Give the people what they are dying to see.

Erika looked at her daughter. She could see the pain splashed across her face. She leaned forward and squeezed her daughter's hand. "I don't condone what you did, but it will get better. All of this will blow over."

"Not if I can't graduate with my friends," Delilah said. She didn't even know if she had friends at this point. It must suck knowing that you were the sidekick, and you were tossed to the side like last season's fashion. We would say Danielle would pick you up proudly and wear you, but she can't afford it now.

"Keep your head in the sand the next couple of weeks, and you'll get through it. I know you have a fighter inside of you."

Delilah looked at her mother. She knew her mother had no clue how Johnson Prep worked. Danielle put a knife in her back, and she didn't kill her. Now it was time for Delilah to destroy her once best friend. "I'll make sure to come out stronger on this. You don't have to worry." Delilah balled her fists thinking of everything Danielle did to her.

Delilah, we thought your only talent was being on your knees and whining too much. Are you about to trade in that razor blade for a kitchen knife? We pray to god you didn't become some sad sob story. We got enough of that from Andrew and Jasmine. Do you see them still around? A word of advice; don't even give Danielle a hug when you stab the bitch in the heart. Let her know it was you, and you're no longer the cum-dumpster whore that we all called you now. Boys and girls, act two was about to be even more delicious than act one. We hoped at the end of this bitch war, someone actually spilled blood.

Chapter 2

"You can't be serious," Ethan said, looking at his daughter. "You're actually returning the card?"

Danielle felt proud handing over the credit card to her father. "I don't need it anymore. I don't give a shit if I'm poor."

Ethan laughed and turned to Lily. "You really did a number on our daughter, didn't you?"

Lily smiled. "She's learning that it's better to be a human being than a spoiled brat."

"You're both idiots." He turned back to Danielle. "If you turn me down, then there will be no more parties, no more shopping sprees, or more money." He then turned to Lily. "I'm not giving you anymore allowance. Her school is paid for, but I'm not paying for college."

It looked like daddy was putting his foot down. Danielle, can you handle being fully dirt poor? We saw that your nails could have some work done, but that was just a suggestion from us. Danielle nodded. "I don't want you controlling my life anymore. I ruined friendships trying to keep this image of myself."

Ethan rolled his eyes. "You're such a disgrace."

"Don't talk about our daughter like that. You should be proud she's trying to be an independent girl," Lily said. She couldn't have been more proud of her daughter for sticking up for something she believed in. Lily, we wanted to thank you for making Danielle a better human. We absolutely hated when she backstabbed Delilah to keep her secret safe, or when Dan dumped her because he hated who she was turning into. We heavenly way to see Bethany squirm. We thought we would be in admiration of The Marked Queen, but we had a feeling The Revenged Queen was going to be a much bigger enemy. We hoped you didn't let your self-esteem issues get in the way of ruining her, like she did the rest of your peasant posse. You had a stamp of approval from us. Now get out there and make that cheap, pearl-wearing bitch cry.

"Then you're nothing more than the dumb slut. Jordan, we are Caraway girls. We believe in fun, but we believe in burning that house down. Are you going to be some weak thing?"

Jordan stood up and looked at her sister. "I am the Revenged Queen. You should have seen her face when I texted her, but it was just a bluff."

"It sounds to me that you might have bluffed about her secrets, but if she looked scared, then she had something to worry about." Val kissed her sister on the cheek. "Stop worrying about putting a cock in your mouth and take the throne. You'll be a senior next year, and you need to show the other's why you deserve to be at the top. Danielle clearly failed, and you better not." She walked over to the door.

"You're leaving?" Jordan asked.

Val turned. "I have people needing me. Have fun alone in the castle. Maybe you can find a boy not afraid of some rumors." She winked and walked out of the room. We had to admit that Val could be our favorite of the new characters introduced. She seemed like a heartless bitch, and she learned how to perfect her craft. We cheer a lollipop to you, girl.

Jordan walked out of her room and down the stairs into the living room. She walked over to look at the city lights from their condo. Her parents were gone, and she had the whole place to herself. She texted a couple of guys to see if they wanted to come over, but none of them accepted. She knew her reputation had been tarnished because of Bethany.

She felt a couple of tears fall from her eyes. She gripped her phone and threw it across the room. She hated the silence more than anything else. Jordan, we didn't want you to be some pathetic sob story. That was what Andrew and Jasmine were for. We thought we got rid of the sad sacks, and we just wanted cunts. Get your shit together girl, because it's time for you to be The Revenged Queen. You wanted Bethany to pay for what she did, and now, it was time for you to do it. Don't worry, you would have some allies soon enough, our new queen.

Chapter 5

Calvin thought it was odd holding another man's hand. He found it different to be looking into someone's eyes. He didn't know how to feel knowing he was on a date with someone that wasn't Aman. Calvin, we didn't want you to be upset. At least, you can be out in the open with this boy.

Terrell leaned back and smiled at Calvin. "Are you having a good time?" he asked.

Calvin smiled. "Yes."

Terrell raised an eyebrow. "Are you over him?" He wasn't sure Calvin was ready to date so soon. He thought he was cute, but he knew the red flags were around him.

Don't worry Terrell, we also knew you weren't looking for someone serious. We heard you just wanted your raging boner to not get blue balled.

"Of course I'm over him," Calvin said.

Calvin, you didn't need to lie to us, sweetie. We knew damn well you cried while jerking off to his naked photo this morning like some sad fag. We get that you miss the brown, but you were trying to upgrade? Least Terrell didn't have that tacky beard, and we're not talking about Aman's facial hair.

"It's okay if you aren't. I get that you have a lot of leftover feelings for him."

Calvin was annoyed that they were talking about his ex on their first date. "I spent weeks, even months, trying to get him to come out. He decided against it. I saw a side of him that I wasn't proud of."

"But you came out after all of it," Terrell said. He reached over and glided his fingers down Calvin's forearm. "I must say it would have been nice sneaking around."

It sent a shiver down Calvin's spine. "I doubt that you would have enjoyed it for too long."

Terrell smirked. "I do have a thing for cars." He winked.

Calvin blushed. Calvin wasn't used to having someone so forward.

We wanted to imagine your sex life with Aman, but it was probably him praying after he was done screwing you. "I wouldn't mind seeing if the backseat of your car has enough room."

Terrell leaned forward. "Are you saying we should get out of here?" he asked.

Calvin leaned forward into Terrell's bubble. "Why are we still wasting time?"

They grabbed the check and walked out of the restaurant. They got into Terrell's car and drove toward a local park. It wasn't terribly late at night, but there wouldn't be spectators, unless they wanted an audience for this train wreck.

Calvin thought the whole time about how to please Terrell. He didn't know if he would like the same things that Aman did. He didn't know if he was going to be good enough for Terrell. Calvin, you were a hot, young bottom. Of course, you were Terrell's type. You just didn't know that he loved to use you as his cum drop off and walk away from your ass.

Terrell and Calvin parked the car. Calvin turned to Terrell, who had hunger in his eyes. Terrell leaned forward and grabbed Calvin's shirt. He pulled him in and their lips crushed together. Calvin wasn't used to someone being so forceful, but he wasn't going to complain.

They felt themselves getting hard and more into it. "Get into the backseat now," Terrell demanded.

Calvin, as a good bottom, got out of the car and went into the back of the car. Terrell walked over to Calvin's side of the car. Calvin was laying on his back, but Terrell didn't like looking at his slam pieces. He leaned down and kissed Calvin one more time. He then flipped him over.

Calvin wasn't used to being on his stomach. He felt Terrell unbuckling his pants and pulling them down. He wanted to say something about prep, and that there should be more of foreplay. He didn't want to come off as someone that couldn't just stick it in. Calvin, there was nothing wrong with having a tight ass. We just hoped you knew how to keep it clean once Terrell was done with you.

Calvin felt a ball of nerves when he heard Terrell unbuckling his panks. He felt Terrell's hands on his ass. Calvin gave out a little yip when Terrell slapped him on the ass. Calvin wanted to protest. He felt like this was wrong, but he didn't get a chance.

He felt pain at first, but then he felt the pleasure of Terrell going in. He grabbed on the seat as he let out a moan. He felt Terrell continue to thrust inside of him, and he felt pleasure from him. He wanted it to continue forever. He had never felt like this with Aman. They were out in the open fucking, and he wanted it to continue.

Terrell felt himself getting close. He enjoyed Calvin's tight ass, and this was why he prayed on the young and innocent. He enjoyed playing the good guy, when really he just wanted to get inside their pants. He hoped Calvin didn't turn into a closet case.

He felt his phone go off. He knew Calvin wouldn't notice. That was why he was on his stomach. We wanted to give you a round of applause for multitasking. We see the text was from another horny bottom that you were just dying to get inside of. We didn't know where you kept up the stamina.

Terrell got off. He stepped back and pulled off the condom. He threw it into the woods and pulled his pants up and fixed himself.

Calvin felt motionless. He had never been fucked like that, and he was in a state of ecstasy. He slowly got up and pulled his pants up to fix himself. He turned to Terrell. "That was amazing." He leaned forward to get a kiss.

Terrell turned him down. "Listen, this was fun, but I got to go. Someone else is in need of my services."

"What?" Calvin, this was the version of fucking Terrell did best. He made you believe you could be more than a slam piece, but he only gave them a meal and a dessert.

Terrell smiled. "I don't do commitment or clingy guys. You're not over your ex, and I'm not looking to be a fill in." Terrell patted him on the shoulder. "The sex was good. You could loosen up though." He winked.

Terrell walked toward the driver side. Calvin felt completely crushed at that moment. "How do you expect me to get home?"

"You're rich, and you have a phone. It's called using Uber." He got into his car and drove away.

Calvin, you were turning into Jasmine, making all the guys run away. We hoped this didn't turn into a pattern. You were left fucked and used. You should have learned that in the gay world, guys don't get close to other guys. They play for the dick, not the heart. We hoped this was a perfect introduction into being out, because we had a feeling Terrell wasn't going to be the only one dumping and running.

Chapter 6

My, my, my, our sweet Susan. We heard the reason you transferred was a little breakdown. Now, what would happen if the whole school found out about your starring role? We didn't know Fiddler On The Roof was meant to have a nude scene. Watch your pills carefully, because I'm dying to see an encore performance. -The Revenged Queen.

Susan saw the note in her locker, and she felt her heart drop to the ground. She looked around to see if it was anyone she knew. She trusted that Bethany would protect them from these attacks. She crumpled up the note and shoved it in her bookbag.

Jordan purposely walked by when Susan was shoving the note in her bookbag, and bumped into her. Susan's things dropped to the ground. Jordan, we knew you were the woman to send the note, and now, you were being violent. We had to admit, you were more of a bully than The Marked Queen.

"Sorry, I didn't see you there."

Susan bent down to grab her things. "It's fine. I have a lot on my mind."

Jordan crossed her arms. "What's that? You're feeling guilty for exposing to the world that I love sex?"

Susan looked at up at Jordan and stood up. "I was never in charge of your secrets. I was supposed to find dirt on Jasmine. She was my best friend, and I just wanted her to come back."

Jordan laughed. "Or, maybe Jasmine found out your dirty secret."

"What?" Susan looked confused. She thought for a moment that Jordan might be the Revenged Queen.

Jordan, you were getting cocky, and that would be your downfall. You really thought you were invincible, but you didn't get any goodnight calls from your family last night. The only positive convo you had yesterday was with a private investigator. "Why else would Jasmine be so mean to you? You must have done something shameful."

"I don't know what you're talking about. I'm not like the rest of you girls. I have no secrets to hide."

"Right." Jordan made her voice extend the ending of the word. "Have fun trying to prove to the world that you aren't a massive bitch for ruining people's lives. Susan, you should know that you're swimming with sharks." Jordan looked Susan up and down. "It's going to be sad seeing Nemo get eaten alive." Jordan waved and walked away from her. She took in a deep sigh because she knew that she could have blown it right then.

Susan felt her emotions take the best of her. She left her medication at home, but she needed some reassurance from Bethany. She ran toward the photography room. She walked in to see Bethany and Tucker going over some of his photography. You would think for being the newly crowned king and queen, they wouldn't still be so fucking boring. Why not fuck in the photography room? Bethany, are you afraid you might make another mistake? Oh dear, we said too much already.

"I got this in my locker today. Susan slammed it on the desk. "There is a new queen trying to come after us. What if it's someone that we exposed?" she asked.

Bethany picked up the piece of paper and looked at it. "Really, The Revenged Queen? She could have been original."

"Do you think we have something to worry about?" Tucker asked.

"People are going to threaten us. We have to stay strong, and it will blow over."

"But what if they use this against me? Bethany, I can't..." Susan began to say.

Bethany slapped her across the face. "You need to calm down. This is how it all falls apart. We knew people would come for us. If you want to keep this secret in the closet then you show no weakness."

Susan held her cheek and ignored the pain. She shook her head. "Or I completely lay low and away from this." She grabbed her things and walked out of the room. She wouldn't have her secret exposed. She couldn't be the laughing-stock of the school. Susan, we wanted to see what kind of crazy you had under your hood.

"Do you think that was necessary?" Tucker asked.

Bethany fixed her basic-ass hair. "She needs to calm down. We are going to get threats, and we need to ignore them. We rule this school, and it's our job to keep it that way."

"So, you've never heard of this Revenged Queen until today?" Tucker asked.

"No, and she's smart enough to not to attack me." Bethany, you just lied to the one guy that truly had your back. Maybe that was why the drama between you in the cafeteria would eventually happen. "Did you get anything?"

Tucker shook his head. "No, I haven't."

She picked up her things. She leaned forward and kissed Tucker on the lips. "Then we will be fine. It's just someone trying to get Susan to turn. I'll make sure she keeps quiet." She waved Tucker off as she left the room.

Bethany, you stupid queen. Susan wasn't going to be the one you had to fear. It was so damn hard to see true love become true betrayal. Tucker pulled out his note from The Revengeful Queen. He was worried that everything they tried to accomplish with The Marked Queen would be a huge fail.

You might have wanted us all to forget, but how could we? I hope while looking at this photo, you sleep tonight remembering what you accomplished. Tucker, you thought you were invincible by dating The Marked Queen, but that made you my favorite target. Go after the bitch's heart. Enjoy knowing your masterpiece photograph was still your mugshot. – The Revenged Queen.

Tucker crumbled up the photo of Elizabeth, and he buried the emotions he had right then. He hoped his girlfriend was right about this being a scare tactic, because he wouldn't be the one going down for this. He agreed with The Marked Queen that people need to forget about Elizabeth, and not be reminded of her.

You should have thought about that before entering your pathetic self into a full-blooded bitch war. You were now sitting at the throne, and you had to be the guillotine yourself. Only question was, would it be by public opinion or guilt for murder?

Chapter 7

"So, why'd you call?" Christian asked, taking a sip of his scotch. Danielle and him were in his limo on their way to dinner. Could Christian be any sexier? He still looked like our wet dream, but he had to add a Tom Ford suit to the mix. Then his dark hair was slicked back, showing his beautiful blue eyes, and he was rocking a beard. Damn, did our panties get wet.

"I'm broke."

Christian raised an eyebrow. He laughed and shook his head. "You're an idiot for giving up the money."

"I wanted to be happy as myself."

"How did that work out for you?" he asked.

"We might be homeless," Danielle said.

"The queen of the Upper East Side is now going to be the queen of the gutters. That's an ironic twist."

"You don't have to be an ass," Danielle said.

"I'm having some fun. I told you that money was all you needed in life. You had to give up a little bit of your dignity and morals for it."

"I backstabbed a friend and lost my boyfriend because of it. I didn't like who I was becoming," she said.

He waved her off. "Listen, I had my moral high road stint also. My dad cut me off as well. I wanted to continue to travel the world, and I didn't know how I was going to pay for it," he said. Christian, we would have given you the money ourselves if you just took off your shirt. Oh wait, we heard that was how you continued your hobbies.

"How did you still travel?" she asked.

He pulled out a card from his pocket. He now invested in the website that gave him his safety net. Christian wanted to think he was disgusted by what he did, but he loved every second of it. He learned the fucked-up realty of this world, and it made him heartless, not stupid. "Call this number."

She took the card. "Fetish.com?" She looked at him. "What in the world is this?"

He laughed. He learned forward and did a line of cocaine. He thought it was interesting that even in New York City, there was still a sense of innocence. He was going to lead this little red riding hood straight to the stripper pole. "It's exactly what you think. There's a whole world of people willing to pay good money to have their fantasies lived out on screen."

She felt disgusted holding this card. She didn't know why Christian would suggest it. "I won't sell my body for some creeps." She thought about people loving used panties and feet.

He rolled his eyes. "You're poor. You don't get to have any kind of judgment. You're desperate for the cash. You don't have to have sex with them. There's legit a section where you wear lingerie and clean the house."

"What did you do?" Danielle asked. She was curious what made him so accepting of this website.

Christian laughed. "I just showed off my body. I made sure I wore skimpy shorts, and I worked out. I even sold my underwear." We felt jealous of the man that purchased any product from you.

"And you didn't feel ashamed."

"Once again, stop acting like the world is filled with rainbows. You continue to indulge in the pure side of the world. It's so much more fun on the dark side. You made the mistake of giving up the money the first time. You're about to be homeless. You called me knowing it wasn't going to be one hundred percent pure."

Danielle looked at the card, and she knew he was right. She knew Christian could get her the cash she needed to save her family. She didn't want to be homeless, but it felt wrong. Danielle, you've always destroyed people's lives. Was taking off your clothes any worse? We wanted you to have another scandal on your hands, especially since Delilah wanted to take you the fuck down.

"I'll give them a call," Danielle said.

Christian raised a glass. "Welcome to the family."

They drove to dinner knowing that their friendship was about to blossom even more. Danielle, we hoped Dan would be okay with this, but we had a feeling your annoying stable boy would change your mind. We were curious if you planned to tell him, but only time would tell. It looked like everyone forgot their lessons from prom, and that made it even more delicious for the reckoning at graduation.

Chapter 8

"Emily?" Tucker asked. He had come to The Pocket to talk to her. He knew that her father owned this bar, and he felt she was the only one that he could trust. What does the photographer want with the bad girl? Did Emily just find her new victim?

Emily turned to see Tucker standing there. She laughed. "What do you want?"

"I wanted to talk to you."

"Why not talk to your girlfriend? You and her had choice words about me when I was dating Andrew," Emily said. She remembered how much Tucker and Bethany didn't want Andrew to have anything to do with her. Well, in their defense, you did cause his meltdown, his relapse, and his second stint in rehab.

"Because she won't understand like you do."

She looked at him. "And what's that?"

"Matthew," he said.

Her face faltered and she turned away from him. "I have nothing to talk about when it comes to that. Besides, how do I know you won't run to The Marked Queen about it?"

"Because I need your help. You were able to move past Matthew, and I can't get over Elizabeth."

She looked at him. "Who is Elizabeth?"

"She's the woman I killed a year ago."

She looked at Tucker, and she remembered vaguely that happening. "Ah, you're the one they called Tucking Killer."

He rolled his eyes. "You would think with their wealth that they could have come up with a better nickname, if you asked me."

Emily laughed. She signaled for the bartender to bring them shots. "If you're going to hangout, you might as well get drunk."

"Just know, I'm a recovering alcoholic."

She shrugged. "Hey, you wouldn't be the first one. Besides, didn't you know? I like corrupting the young and bright and killing them." She raised the shot glass to him. They took a shot to their disparity. We needed a drink for all this depression. We wanted a bitch story, not a melodrama.

"What happened?" Tucker asked.

"I didn't even get him into drugs. I was some punk girl, but I wasn't into the drugs and alcohol. I would go to concerts all of the time because I was so obsessed with music. I met Matthew at a random dive bar. There was a shitty band playing, but I wanted to hear them. Matthew was there by himself. I knew who he was because he was the quarterback of the football team."

"So, you didn't corrupt him?"

"No, he loved his drugs, and I fell for it. He told me I was special, and I got involved. We would get drunk and high all the time. I let it consume me, while I felt like he was just getting started. I could never keep up with him. I didn't know what he was trying to run away from."

"So, what happened that night?" Tucker asked.

Emily looked at him. She hadn't really told people this story. She closed her eyes, and she let the tears begin to fall. She wanted nothing more than to forget about all of this. She wished she never went to that hotel. "Matthew wanted to meet up, and I agreed. He sounded fucked up already."

"I walked into that hotel room, and he was already gone. He had started before me. He talked about pushing his limits, but I never thought he would."

"Wait, you weren't even there when he died?" Tucker asked. People made it seem like she forced the needle in his arm.

She laughed. "I looked like the punk rock girl, and people could never assume the All-American boy could do that to himself. They all blamed me. I got tainted as the bad news bitch. I see how the seniors look at me. They were all friends with him, and they had no clue what he was really like."

"And things were made worse with Andrew."

"I attract the crazies, and they let their demons out to play with me. I'm still the horrible bitch that killed one and sent the other to rehab." She took another shot.

"How do you deal with it? I was drunk, and I regret killing her. I should have gone to jail for what I did. I'm tired of being this victim to the stigma."

"Is that why you were part of The Marked Queen?"

Tucker nodded. "I don't regret it, but it didn't accomplish what I wanted it to." He pulled out the note The Revenged Queen gave him. "People still see me as the guy that killed that woman."

Emily looked at the note, and she saw it was Jordan's handwriting. Emily laughed on the inside. She knew her best friend would eventually get her revenge, and she was surprised she worked this quick. She looked at Tucker, and sympathized with him. He knew what it was like to be the town's villain.

"You'll find a friend that won't judge you," she said.

Tucker smiled. "I need that."

They cheered to their new friendship. Tucker, we hoped Bethany was okay with you being friends with the enemy. It seemed new alliances were being formed, and we wondered what would happen to this new one. We hoped Bethany and Jordan found out. You two were about to be bargaining chips for both of our queens. One question we had was, who would go with who?

Chapter 9

Calvin had struck out for the third consecutive time. He tried to keep his anger to a minimum, but this was the quarterfinals. He didn't want to let his team down. He tried to forget about being left in the park by Terrell. A guy left in the dust, why does that seem so familiar?

Calvin turned to see Aman and Sana in the stands. Oh yeah, Aman left you in the dust for another bitch. It must suck seeing them all happy together. Is that why you weren't playing your best? Calvin gripped the bat as hard as he could, when the umpire announced that he was out.

"Better luck next time, faggot," the catcher said.

Calvin turned to look at him. "Excuse me?" Calvin got into his face. His team had no problem that he was gay. They welcomed him with open arms. He wasn't expecting another team to bash him.

The catcher got up and took off his helmet. "Maybe you should work on your swing over your dick sucking. We know you don't have what it takes to be a baseball player."

Calvin laughed. "You're right. Maybe I should be a boxer instead." Calvin balled his fist up and punched the guy across the face with all his force.

The guy fell back. The two teams saw what happened and came to their teammates defense. These boys and their emotions. We thought women were hysterical. We hoped they take their shirts off. Who doesn't love sweat, blood, and abs?

The catcher tried to punch Calvin back, but Calvin was protected by his teammates. The coaches and umpires broke up the fight, much to our disappointment. We wanted someone to seriously get injured. Paul and Audrey looked for their son, and they were worried for him. They knew he had a lot issues since Aman dumped his ass, and they knew it wasn't easy seeing him here.

The umpire ejected Calvin and the catcher from the game. Calvin sat in the locker room trying to compose himself. He shook his head and cried. He didn't know what was wrong with him. He felt all over the place, and he needed to calm his nerves.

He knew Ian liked to have a couple of shots before the game started. He opened Ian's locker and grabbed his duffel bag. He found the bottle of vodka, and he took a couple of swigs. He felt himself relaxing. Calvin, we didn't want you to turn into Andrew. We get that alcohol could be fun, but it didn't solve your problems.

"You just got in a fight on the field, and now you're drinking," Coach Soto said, walking into the locker room. He left his assistant coach in charge of the game while he checked on Calvin.

"I just took a shot. I wasn't drunk on the field."

Coach Soto came to sit next to Calvin. "You could have fooled me with the performance you just displayed on the field. I know you got a lot of shit going on. Why not tell me what's the issue?"

"You would think it would be easier being out. The team doesn't give a shit, but I couldn't with that guy. He deserved to be punched in the face."

"You can't punch everyone that calls you a homophobic slur."

"He deserved it," Calvin said. Calvin wasn't going to sit there and be bashed for what he did. He would do it all over again because it felt fucking right.

Coach Soto sighed. "What else is going on?" he asked.

Calvin didn't care if he was going to get in trouble. He took another sip from the bottle. Coach Soto took it from him. "You don't get to be drunk right now."

Calvin turned. "Why not? I lost my boyfriend, a guy fucked me in the park and left me there, and I punched an asshole for calling me a faggot. I think things are going well for me right now, don't you?" Calvin asked. Well, we found our train wreck this time around. Hoped you make as epic a performance as Andrew did at prom.

Coach Soto opened his mouth then shut it. He didn't know what to say. "I'm sorry a lot of shit is coming your way right now. You have your baseball career." He paused. "Or maybe you won't."

"What's that supposed to mean?"

"I have to meet with the school board after this incident. You might not be able to play the remainder of the year."

"Why not?" Calvin stood up. "He started it with a fucking slur."

"But you hit him. We don't accept violence on the field. If you have aggression, you should have played football." He stood up. "Grab the rest of your stuff. Your parents are outside waiting for you." He looked down at the bottle of vodka. "I won't tell them about this."

"Why not? They're too loving to see their son is a fucking mess," Calvin said, while grabbing his things. He walked outside of the locker room to see his parents standing there. Audrey grabbed him first. "Are you okay?" she asked.

"He called me a faggot, and I wasn't going to let him get away with it," Cavin said.

Paul looked at his son with a stern expression. "But I hope it was worth possibly ruining your baseball career."

"Dad, I ruined my baseball career when I realized that I loved the taste of cock," he replied.

None of them said anything after Calvin's statement. They walked away from the game, trying to put this behind them. Calvin, we thought you were supposed to be happy you were out of the closet. You could have anyone you wanted, well, not everyone. It was tragic to see that it doesn't get better when you accept who you truly are, because you had to be accepted by everyone else around you. Calvin, you were zero for two. We just wondered if that number would continue. Good luck finding love in booze and boys.

Chapter 10

Delilah just got out of her lovely after school class. It was three hours of bullshit, in her eyes. Delilah, you should have learned that sucking the wrong cock has consequences. We should look at Principal Grand. He was too busy running from the cops. We hoped you thought it was worth giving him your cherry pie. We enjoyed the scandal.

Delilah turned the corner to see Jordan and Carter were talking. "I'll give you whatever money you want, if you hack her fucking school records."

Carter rolled his eyes. He had enough of these spoiled girls trying to get something from him. "I told you that I was done doing that."

Carter, we were surprised that you had a colorful past. We assumed the only thing interesting about you was when you were in love with the fat girl.

"Please, you didn't get caught."

"But I almost did," Carter said. Carter tried to hack the college admissions board to see if he got accepted into Stanford, but he almost got caught by the police..

"It's Johnson Prep, not Stanford. No one is going to give a shit," Jordan said, handing him an envelope of cash.

Carter shook his head. "You really think you can just wave your money to get whatever you want."

"She deserves to go down," Jordan said. She knew Carter wouldn't reveal her identity, because he didn't care about social standings. "I thought you would be down after she went after your girlfriend," she said.

Carter turned to see Delilah standing there. "No." He walked away from her without giving her a chance to respond.

Jordan turned to see Delilah standing there. "What was all that about?" Delilah asked.

She smiled. "Nothing you need to worry about," she said. She tried to walk past her. She didn't know much about Delilah, minus the principal scandal.

Delilah grabbed her arm. "Who are you going after?" she asked.

Jordan looked at her. "None of your business. It's not your type of fun."

"If you remember, I'm the one that took down Flynn."

She laughed. "Flynn was an easy target. I'm going after a much bigger bitch."

Jordan thought for a moment. Jordan was exposed by The Marked Queen also. "You're going after Bethany. That's bold."

"Exactly. I don't need people to be weak when it comes to her."

Delilah laughed. "Please, she had Tucker and Susan. I doubt that I'm weaker than them."

Jordan knew Delilah had a good point. She looked at Delilah. She knew she had a lot of anger inside of her. She was exposed as the principal's slam piece, and her best friend backstabbed her. She knew she needed some help when it came to Bethany. She crossed her arms. "Why do you want in?"

"You have no clue the look of shame I've gotten from everyone around me. I was some dumb girl to them. It was confirmed when it was exposed that I was sleeping with the principal. I wanted to be known for my writing, but that won't happen anymore. That bitch thinks she's better than everyone else."

"We were both slut shammed for things we didn't want to be shammed for. I love dick, and I shouldn't be bashed for it."

Jordan, you were such a strong feminist character. We hoped little girls looked up to you.

"Bethany isn't the only bitch I want to go after. I want in, but I want Danielle to go down too," Delilah said. She was so tired of Danielle getting away with murder. She still felt the sting of betrayal from her best friend. She had always been there for her, and Danielle tossed her to the side like she meant nothing.

Jordan raised an eyebrow. "You really hate her that much?"

"She sold me out instead of Calvin. Fuck both of them."

Jordan thought about it. Why make it just about Bethany? She knew that Delilah would be a great asset, because of the rage she saw behind her eyes. She knew that this would get messy, and she needed an ally. "So, there's bad blood between you two?" We hoped someone played that Taylor Swift song, so these two would be inspired.

Delilah got into her face. "I hate that bitch with all my heart."

"This is going to be fun," Jordan said. "I want to rule this school."

Oh look, another girl with no real friends trying to be loved by the masses. What was with you girls at Johnson Prep? Why couldn't you just love yourselves? Oh wait, this was a ruthless book. We didn't do heartfelt here. We assumed those dick-less nights has made you a bitter bitch, Jordan.

"I hope it does. I want to take all of them down. It's time for them to have slut or whore sprayed across their lockers. I want them to be looked at like the mistake of their family," Delilah said. She still hadn't heard from her father, and she knew he was keeping his distance from her.

Jordan smiled and put out her hand. "Welcome to the team of The Revenged Queen. We only have one mission here."

Delilah took her hand and shook it. "Let's burn this fucking building down."

A new alliance has been formed, and it looked like their targets had no idea what they were about to get. Bethany, we hoped you enjoyed your two seconds on the throne. We were just pleased you kept it warm for us. We hoped you knew how to retaliate, but we had a feeling your cards were about to be shown. Danielle, why couldn't you have taken the high ground and backstabbed both of your friends? Maybe then your fate wouldn't have turned out so tragic. The storm was brewing, and we could guarantee one thing, not everyone would survive the night of graduation. We just wanted to know who would.

Chapter 11

"Pregnant?" Bethany asked, looking at the doctor. My, my, Bethany, you were bringing us an heir to the kingdom. We thought Danielle was supposed to act like trailer park trash. We guessed that you had really fucked up your morals. Who knew Tucker and you did the dirty deed? We just all thought your form of intercourse was holding each other's hands.

"I would say you're about five to six weeks," Dr. Melissa said. She walked over and sat down next to her. "There are options we can discuss if you would like."

Bethany turned to her doctor. "There's only one option. I want to abort it." Bethany knew that this baby would ruin everything about her future. She also knew that it would be humiliating when she went off to Brown about to pop. Bethany, you could blame it on the freshman fifteen. We also needed you to realize no one would give a shit about you in college.

"Are you sure about this? It's a huge decision."

Bethany sat up. She turned and looked at her doctor. "I'm going to Brown in the fall. I will not have some mistake ruin my life." She got off the table.

"Do you want to discuss this with the father of the child?"

Bethany thought about what she would say to Tucker. She knew he was too fragile right now. She knew something had spooked him, and he was all over the place. She found out from a source that he was hanging out with Emily. She couldn't put this on him.

"He's out of the picture." How true would those words would be in the future? Bethany, he wasn't one of your worshippers, but you would soon learn that.

"What day did you want to perform the procedure?"

"As soon as possible. Let's do next week," Bethany said.

Dr. Melissa walked out of the room to look at booking the appointment. Bethany sighed when she left the room. She shook her head, and she tried to keep it together. She was shaking. She clung to her stomach, for some odd reason, she wanted to keep this child. She has always wanted children, but she knew she was too young.

She stood up. Her mother raised her with elegance. She was a Winchester after all. She was supposed to change this world, not end up on welfare. She would pay whatever she had to make sure this was all put to rest.

Dr. Melissa walked back into the room. "You're all set for next Friday."

Bethany walked toward the door. "Thank you so much," she said, as she walked out the door and outside the building, quickly getting into her town. She thought about how she would tell Tucker, but she wouldn't until it was over with.

She got to her townhouse, and she wanted to sleep. Yes, it must have been exhausting knowing that you're beneath all of your peasants. The Marked Queen slutting it up. We thought that was for Jordan; not you. We also knew that it looked like everyone was switching roles in this school. You flipped everyone on their heads except for you. It looked like you were flipped on your back.

She opened the front door to see her mother cleaning the stairs. "Mom, what are you doing?" Bethany asked.

Bethany's mother, Linda turned and smiled. She was the same ordinary woman that Bethany was. She had flat brown hair, pasty skin complexion, and green eyes that looked like grass. The one thing Linda had over her daughter was heart.

"Honey, you know I don't trust the maids to clean the stairs properly. Plus, I want them to have some rest." Linda walked over and pulled her daughter into a hug.

Bethany felt safe in her mother's arms. It was nice to be in a parent's arm. Her father had passed away when she was younger. It was a plane crash, and it was all over the news. What was with you girls and having no father figures? Was this why you were all such ruthless harlots?

Linda looked at her daughter. "You look tired. Is everything all right?"

Bethany wanted to tell her mother, but how could she? She didn't want her mother to know how much of a disappointment she has been lately. "I just had a long day with committees and everything."

"You're almost done. Only a couple weeks till graduation, then you're off to Brown. I can't believe my baby girl is growing up."

"I'm trying to live my glory days of high school. I'm making memories to last a lifetime."

Linda smiled. She was so worried when Bethany didn't have any girlfriends to hang out with. She was pleased she was with Tucker, but he was a bit of a wallflower. She wanted her daughter to go to all the football games, dances, and remember these times with friends. Aw Linda, your daughter was making memories for herself. Did she tell you how she exposed everyone's secrets at school, ruined so many people's lives, and now, she got herself pregnant? We didn't think she would forget about these memories anytime soon.

"Yes, I am. I just need to go lay down," Bethany said. She walked up the stairs and into her room and closed the door. She went for the bed. She laid down, and turned her head into the pillows. She began to cry. She had let her mom down, and she knew she wouldn't look at her the same. Bethany, if it made you feel better, your father wasn't here to be disappointed. Your mother was too nice to tell you to your face how you disrespected the family's name.

It was truly tragic when the one cold-hearted bitch turned out to be another low self-esteem sob story. We hoped you gained some of your confidence back, or The Revenged Queen was going to eat you alive. You had better continue holding that mistake — we mean "buddle of joy." We had a feeling this dirty secret was going to be out quicker than your abortion. You were no longer The Marked Queen we were inspired by, but every queen needs a new name. Isn't that right, Shotgun Wedding Queen.

***

Lights, camera, and a little bit of skin. It looked like our favorite girl knew how to pose for the camera. She knew damn well how to bat her eyelashes and give those horny boys a little wet dream for later. Danielle, you were coming a long way from the spoiled brat you were before.

You were standing in front of the camera, dancing around with a black lace bra and panties on. She had her hair curly, and she was nothing more than seductive. You wanted those bills paid, girl, then you needed to slut your body to get it. We want to hand you a crisp one hundred just to see what you would do for it.

She ignored the comments from the gentlemen in the chat trying to get her to take off her clothes. She smiled. "Maybe next time." She winked, and that sent on a slew of comments about how sexy her wink was.

She stood up and danced around showing her ass off. We never knew our rich girl would become a stripper, but it seemed like the course she was willing to take. Danielle, we hoped this was worth going to college. Who were we kidding? You weren't going to college now. You would be known as the internet whore. Hoped you had a high price tag!

She looked over at the clock and knew Dan would be here any moment. "Boys, I hate to cut this short. I'll see you next week." She winked and closed her laptop. She ran into her room to put on a robe.

Dan walked into her room a couple of seconds later. "Did you decide to get comfortable?" Dan asked.

Danielle smiled and turned around for him. "I thought I would look cute for you." She was really looking good for her sea of horny worshippers. You thought you were the only one seeing those goods?

Dan walked over and kissed her on the cheek. "You could never be anything else."

She leaned forward and captured his lips with hers. She wanted to forget about all the men that told her dirty things. She knew that it was for her to keep a roof above their heads. We knew deep down that you loved the attention all these men were giving you. They were willing to throw their money, just to see what you would do for them. Danielle, it had been so long since anyone has wanted to throw money at you for sex. We had bet if you sat on the street with a poverty sign, you would get a couple of dollars, but The Revenged Queen would use it against you.

"You're too sweet."

Dan looked at her. "You nervous about not having money?" he asked. He wondered how her time in the poverty lane would be.

She smiled and shook her head. "I just have a lot going on that's all." Danielle had to postpone her interview with Parson's so that she could do this video. She knew this money would be enough to cover some of the back rent.

"You're interview went well. You'll get in." He wrapped his arms around her. "You have so much talent."

Dan, we really wished you would learn how to stop being so stupid. We understood you saw the world in rainbows and butterflies. That was fine for a five-year-old girl, but you lived in New York. That won't cut it in this city. Your girlfriend's only talent was showing her skin off to half hard cocks covered in lube and old man tears.

"Thank you, babe. Do you want to get dinner started?" she asked. She needed to call Christian and see what he thought.

Danielle, why didn't you do a collaboration video with him? We just wanted to see our favorite hotties naked and wild. You were already doing soft core porn.

He nodded. "I love you."

She touched the side of his face. She hated keeping this from him. Her secrets last time killed their relationship, and she didn't want to do it again. She smiled. "I love you, too."

He walked out of the room to cook dinner. She pulled out her phone and called Christian. "I have to say that I made a deposit in your honor," Christian said, when he picked up. He watched her show, and he wouldn't deny his arousal. He played with his fun stick.

Danielle rolled her eyes. "Do you think it's going to be enough to cover back rent?"

"You're going to be a new sensation. I can't wait to see where this takes you."

"Danielle, I need your help in the kitchen," Dan screamed.

"I just don't want my boyfriend to find out," Danielle said. "I'll be right there," she screamed to Dan.

Christian laughed. "When are you going to get rid of that wet blanket? He's going to hold you back in life. You weren't meant for the ordinary. Once you realize that humbling yourself was such a drag, you should call me." Christian hung up because he had a guy over to finish off what Danielle started.

Danielle looked at Christian's number, but she ignored what he had to say. She walked into the kitchen and saw Dan was cooking steak. She walked over and kissed him on the lips. She filled it with passion and heart.

Danielle, you were becoming the stable boy's wife. You weren't meant for the boring life filled with children and happiness. You were dabbling in the dark world, and we wanted you fully. You should have taken Christian's advice. You weren't meant for the ordinary. This was the Upper East Side. You wanted to have kids and be boring, you go to Vermont. It was a bitch world that you thrived in. You had better dump the boy and be the queen bitch we loved in the first place.

Chapter 12

"What do you mean you have to kick me off the team?" Calvin asked. He knew he would get in trouble for punching the guy in the face, but he wasn't expecting this.

Calvin, how far you had fallen? You were the big baseball star, and now we had to look at you like this.

Coach Soto sighed. "I really wish we didn't have to do this, but Johnson Prep has a huge no violence tolerance policy."

Calvin laughed. "But were okay with bullying? Did Bethany get in any trouble for what she pulled at prom?"

Coach Soto didn't say anything at first. "She was given detention for her actions. She shed some light to things that the school board wasn't very aware of."

Calvin rolled his eyes. "Maybe I shouldn't have come out." He closed his eyes, and he felt the tears begin to fall. He wished he just stayed in his lane. He wanted to believe that life would have been better out, but he wasn't so sure.

Coach Soto felt bad for Calvin. He knew that the kid was struggling. He knew that Aman wasn't admitting to his sexuality, and he assumed that it broke Calvin's heart. Coach Soto, you shouldn't feel so bad for Calvin. He did this all to himself. He thought he could wave his rainbow flag without there being any repercussions. It was a fucked-up world we lived in. No one could be themselves without an ignorant asshole ruining it for them.

Calvin looked at Coach Soto. "What do I do now?" he asked. "I've always been known as the baseball star. How do I move forward from this?"

"You have a new identity."

Calvin slammed the desk. "I don't want to be only known as the gay guy." Calvin was a fool to believe that he could have baseball and be gay. He thought that since his teammates accepted him that the world would too.

You were stupid to believe it was going to be easy, Calvin. This was Johnson Prep. There was a new queen in town, and she was damn to make you pay.

"I'm sorry," Coach Soto said. He had no other advice to give him.

Calvin stood up and walked out of that office knowing he was the disgrace of the school now. He walked down the halls, and he saw Aman by his locker. Calvin had only one thing to say to him. He walked right up to him. Aman didn't know what Calvin wanted. He could see he was clearly upset. "You were right to stay in the closet," Calvin said. He walked past Aman after that.

Aman turned to Calvin walking away. It killed Aman's heart to see Calvin this destroyed. He wanted to be there for him, but he didn't know how to. "I'm sorry," Aman whispered. He saw the shell of the man he fell in love with, and he didn't know if the real Calvin would come back.

Calvin walked over to his locker. He opened it to see a letter fall out. He thought he was done with being blackmailed. He picked it up, but it was in a black envelope. "This is new," Calvin said.

He opened the letter.

Poor Calvin, you were supposed to be the top dog on campus. How far the great have fallen. Maybe it has something to do with your friendship with the poor girl. Calvin, you wanted to believe your life would have been better out, than in the closet. How was that working

*out for you? You got anger inside of you. Maybe you shouldn't have
exposed yourself for The Marked Queen. She marked you well, and
you're still on my revenge list. You think the straight males are the
worst to experience. You haven't seen a scorned bitch. Close your eyes
when we pull the trigger because your time at the top has just been cut
short. Good luck in the swamps, fag. -The Revenged Queen.*

Calvin crumpled up the note and threw it in his locker. He
slammed his locker shut, and he punched the locker. He wanted
to get out of this school because he didn't want to see anyone.
He knew everything this new queen said was true. He played
right into The Marked Queen's hand, and he didn't feel
successful.

Delilah and Jordan watched from afar. Delilah was the one
that wrote the note this time. "Do you think fag was necessary?"
Jordan asked.

Delilah turned to look at Jordan. "We were called our
shameful words, why can't he?"

"I thought we were going after Danielle."

Delilah smiled. "We are. Who do you think has her heart?
Dan will come and go. He means nothing to her. Her best friend
does, though. I'm going to make them hate each other. They will
destroy their friendship like Danielle did to me." Delilah knew
it was time for her to burn that alliance.

It seemed that this new queen had some very crafty war
tactics. The Revenged Queen was coming for actual blood, and
we wondered how far they would go. We would be careful if
we were you guys. We all saw how much rage The Marked
Queen brought out of you. Who said no one would be filled
with anger once you were done with your rampage?

Chapter 13

"Here's my test," Delilah said. She handed her Chemistry test to Mr. Rozengota. He had volunteered to proctor all her tests that needed to be reexamined after the Principle Grand scandal came out.

"I'll make sure that it's graded and back to you." He looked back at the test and began going over her answers.

She felt a little infuriated, because he had little contact with her, and it bothered her. "Why aren't you speaking to me?" she asked.

He looked at her. "I don't think my words will be appropriate in this building."

She slammed her hands on the desk. "I've always looked at you as a father figure. You've always been there for me. You gave me the confidence I needed to move forward with my writing. You gave me the strength to expose Flynn. Why can't you help me?"

He looked at her. "Because there's no helping you. You were sleeping with a principal, and I'm so disappointed in you." Mr. Rozengota had no daughters. He had three sons, but he always wanted a daughter. Well, we had the perfect daughter for you. We even heard she had daddy issues. Hopefully, she didn't suck your cock, like she did the last older gentleman.

"You have no clue what I was going through when it all went down."

"What I saw was a person trying to use the system. You tried to take shortcuts, and here we are."

She rolled her eyes. "I did what I needed to make sure that I passed. I'm not going to be ashamed of it," she paused. "I don't want you to hate me." She felt like he filled the void of her missing father. She couldn't lose Mr. Rozengota in this all too.

He stood up and fixed his tie. "I can't accept what you did. It's unforgivable."

"I didn't kill anyone."

"No, but you cheated. I thought you were better than that," Mr. Rozengota said. He wanted nothing more than for her to realize her talent, and he would give her some tough love because she needed it.

She shook her head. "I made mistakes. I won't forget them. I was failing. I thought there was no way that I could survive it." She felt the tears begin to form. "I felt like some stupid whore." Which in your defense, Delilah, you were.

"This is where you get tutoring. This is where you ask for help."

"I did."

"With my boss's dick in your mouth," he snapped. He knew it was extremely inappropriate to say, but he was tired of her excuses.

You had a right to go off on her. We were hoping this was going to happen. We wanted you to tell that bitch she shouldn't have spent so much time her on knees, that people would have thought she was religious.

Delilah nodded. "Is that how you view me now?" she asked. She needed to know the truth. "Am I no longer the girl you were inspired by? I'm no longer your favorite student?"

He didn't say anything more because he went over the line. "I'll make sure this is graded and back to you by tomorrow morning." He grabbed his things and walked out of the room. She was left in the cold by another old man.

Delilah, you might have wanted to think about going for younger guys. It seemed the older ones thought you were too crazy. That was probably why your dad is never home.

***

Susan walked into the room thinking she had study group. She had kept her distance from Bethany and Tucker. She was lying low because she wanted to make sure people didn't come after her. She couldn't get the note The Revenged Queen gave to her out of her head.

Delilah looked up to see Susan there. She was on the revenge list, and she wanted to hit her there. Delilah clapped. "Well done on being the shy girl of the school. You had us all believe you were so sweet."

Susan stopped when she realized Delilah was standing there. "I wanted to go after Jasmine, that's it."

Delilah walked over to her. "But, you didn't just go after Jasmine. You went after all of us."

"Your beef is with Danielle."

Delilah slammed her hand on the desk. "I think my issue is with a lot of people, including you, bitch."

Delilah, you were showing your true colors. Where was this when Principal Grand was dumping your crazy ass?

Susan was startled. "I'm sorry for everything that happened."

Delilah laughed. She knew Susan's real secret. Jordan was the one that told her, and she knew the bitch was crazy. "You want people to believe you're this innocent girl. You want to make people think you have nothing but goodness in your heart."

"I do. I did that to bring Jasmine back to me."

Delilah crossed her arms. "How did that work out? I see from her Instagram that she's in Spain. It must be so hard facing a bitch that backstabbed you."

"I didn't backstab you."

"No, but you gave her the knife and the motive. You three think that you're innocent in all of this. You have no blood on your hands, but that was far from the truth. You put us all in that arena to kill each other. You're worse than all of us."

"What are you going to do about it?" Susan asked. She wanted to know if Delilah was The Revenged Queen.

"Nothing, because karma will come biting you in the ass. I hope your secrets are safe in a fucking vault, because it's time for reckoning on your bullshit ass." She grabbed her books. "Have fun knowing that you're enemy number one." She walked out of the room knowing Susan was about to piss her pants.

Susan took a seat to calm her nerves. She knew that she was regretting more and more getting involved with The Marked Queen. Susan, you shouldn't feel guilty for your actions. They were going to be nothing compared to the ones you would make in the future. No one should back you in a corner.

Chapter 14

"Do you really think a party is necessary?" Delilah asked. She grabbed her glass of champagne and took a sip, all she wanted was to forget everything Mr. Rozengota said to her.

Jordan turned to her new ally and flashed a simple smile. "Of course. You want people to know if they're worthy enough of a Jordan Caraway party."

"I thought everyone came to these," Delilah said.

"That was before that bitch Bethany became The Marked Queen. It's time we show people who they really are." Jordan had a few tricks up her sleeves, and we weren't talking about between the sheets.

Delilah wanted to say something, but she didn't get a chance. There was a knock on the door. Jordan walked over and opened the door to Emily and Tucker. Jordan was delighted to see Emily, but she didn't care for her new friend. She crossed her arms. "Emily, you know he's our enemy."

Emily was expecting this. "He's with me." She leaned forward. "Don't you want to take Bethany's boyfriend away from her? He knows her secrets." Emily wanted her new friend here, because they were bonding over their murders — we mean accidents.

Jordan looked at Tucker. Emily had a fair point. "Fine, but we will discuss later about loyalty."

"Thank you for inviting me over," Tucker said. He knew that he wasn't fully welcomed in this home, and he could understand if Jordan wanted to slam the door in his face.

Emily and Tucker walked toward the back of the apartment for some privacy. "You're letting him in here?" Delilah asked.

Zachary Ryan

"He's part of The Marked Queen kingdom." Delilah wanted to slap him across the face.

Jordan knew Delilah had a lot to learn. Jordan, we could have told you that. Although, you two could bond over sex techniques. She was our dumb bitch last time. We weren't expecting her smarts to grow since then.

"He might be, but haven't you heard about taking an enemy captive? It looks like we just took the bitch's heart."

People started coming to the party. They were dancing and drinking. This was a Jordan Caraway party. She might be The Revenged Queen, but that didn't mean she wasn't the queen of the parties anymore. She knew how to multitask, she was queen of a gang bang, after all.

Shane walked in with a wicked grin. His hair was pulled into a man bun. Yes, even with wealth, there were still douchebags with man buns. He had blue eyes and the devil's smile. "Thanks for the invite."

Jordan smiled. She met him at a rival lacrosse game. "I'm happy you could join." She kissed him on the cheek. "Glad you weren't scared of the rumors."

"That's what intrigued me more to you." He leaned closer to her. "I want to know the wild beast in the bedroom," he whispered.

If that didn't get your panties wet, we didn't know what would. Jordan, you might have found your new love interest. We hoped he turned out good, because with his looks and charm, it seemed like he was more sinister. "I'll see you later." She winked.

Shane and his friends walked to join everyone else. Delilah looked at the guys mingling. "He's cute."

Jordan forgot about Delilah standing there. She turned to look at her. "He's mine, but he does have friends."

"Maybe I should have been friends with you a long time ago," Delilah said. She knew Danielle wouldn't have done anything that sweet for her. Danielle gave you the confidence to talk to Flynn. He then backstabbed you like Danielle. Isn't that what friends were for?

Danielle and Calvin didn't think about what would happen when they walked into Jordan's condo. Danielle wanted to invite Dan, but he wanted to stay at home. She hoped people would eventually get to know him. Danielle, no one cared about your poor ass boyfriend. We just cared about you showing your skin for the camera. You got a mighty big paycheck for your first time. We couldn't wait for more videos. We heard from Christian that you in were high demand.

They walked inside to be stopped by Jordan. "Sorry, we don't let trash in here anymore," Jordan said.

Danielle crossed her arms and raised an eyebrow. "Since when did you not let anyone come inside?"

"Since she learned you're a backstabbing bitch," Delilah said, as she came to walk up next to Jordan.

Danielle's heart dropped. "I'm sorry for what happened. I don't know how many times I have to tell you that."

Calvin grabbed her hand. "You made a mistake, and you shouldn't have to keep paying for it."

Delilah hated seeing Danielle and Calvin be so close. She wished Danielle protected her, but she knew she made her alliance. She was going to destroy that friendship. " It's sad to see how far you both have fallen, but it's so good seeing trash bond with trash."

"You were never this cruel," Danielle said.

"Because I've never been backstabbed before." Delilah shook her head. "I'm tired of this conversation. I have friends to make." She turned and walked away from them.

"You can leave now," Jordan said.

Calvin and Danielle didn't fight it. They walked away and heard the door slam behind them. We thought we would never see the day that Danielle and Calvin were on the blocked list. It seemed as if the times have changed, and we were wondering who would get the throne and keep it. Everyone now had to figure out their ruling in the school, and we wondered where everyone would fall.

****

"I can't believe she kicked us out like that," Danielle said. Danielle and Calvin went to grab burgers after being humiliated. She took a bite of her burger. Yes Danielle, why didn't you become the fat ex-queen? We wouldn't mind seeing you being the butt of everyone's joke.

Calvin took a bite of his burger since it was the only meat he wanted in his mouth right now. "Honestly, I wasn't feeling a party."

Danielle looked at him. She could tell that something was off. She knew about him being kicked off the baseball team. The whole school knew about it the moment it happened. She just didn't know if it was her place to say anything. "Does it have to do with not being on the baseball team?"

He thought about Terrell. He texted the guy multiple times like a fucking idiot. He was being ghosted by the guy that gave him the confidence to come out. Our Sweet Calvin, that was the point of the gay world. They just took what they wanted and left you in the dust once it was all said and done.

"I wish it was just that. A guy turned out to be an asshole to me. We had sex, and he just ghosted me."

Danielle got up and walked over and sat down next to Calvin. She pulled him close to her. "I'm sorry that happened to you," she said. She didn't know what it was like to be used like that, but she didn't enjoy her best friend going through the feelings.

"I thought he would be the perfect guy to show me this world." He felt the tears fall down his face. "I got so angry at that guy calling me a faggot, then seeing Aman and Sana at my game, and then remembering what Terrell did. I just couldn't do it. I let go of so much anger."

"Did you feel better after?" Danielle asked.

Calvin looked at him. "No, I felt worse because now I have nothing." He stood up and walked away from the park bench. He walked in the middle of the field and looked up at the stars; he just wanted there to be some clarity. Calvin, we didn't want you to be a cliché. We get that guys have screwed you over, wasn't that what you were hoping for?

Danielle followed him. "If it makes you feel better, I'm taking my clothes off for money."

Calvin turned around. "Like a stripper."

She laughed. "For a camera. It's a fetish website that Christian got me connected with. I need money for college and making sure we can afford to stay in our home."

"So, your dad really cut you off?" Calvin asked.

She nodded. "I thought he wouldn't let his pride get in the way of taking care of his family. I guess I was wrong. Anyway, you're gay."

"And you're a stripper."

She pulled him into a hug. "I wouldn't have it any other way."

They eventually laid down. "Do you think Delilah will ever forgive me?" she asked.

"She's still pissed at everything you did." Calvin turned to her. "Do you think she's going to seek revenge?"

Danielle knew Delilah. She was too weak to do anything harmful. Oh Danielle, you were going to be in for a rude awakening, and we were ready for it. The girl you used to know is no longer there. Hoped you enjoyed believing you were invincible. You better get all the cash now, before someone found out about your afterschool job.

"I don't know. She looked like she was ready for blood." Calvin paused. "Thank you for never backstabbing me during The Marked Queen days."

"Well, I needed someone in my corner when the chips fell. I wish we were back in those days. It seemed easier."

"Trapped in our secrets." Danielle wished she was still believing she was rich. She was the popular girl that had friends she never betrayed. We didn't want you to go back to being rich. We enjoyed you being desperate and a villain.

"Do you think I'll be loved?" Calvin asked.

Danielle looked at him this time. "Of course."

"No, I mean as a gay man. Do you think I'll find love?"

"I believe so," she said.

"Then why did I have to come out? I found it with Aman. We were so good together. It would have made things easier. My whole life was easier with him in it, and I failed. It doesn't get better as an open gay man."

Danielle grabbed his hand and squeezed it. "You were so miserable in that relationship. You hated baseball because you knew they would reject you."

"But who am I now?" Calvin, please don't be a sad story. You were the guy that guys fucked in the park and tossed you to the side. Although, we wanted to see how much you loved being the slut. Jordan was done with the role, maybe that could be yours now.

"Does anyone ever know who they are? I was the rich girl, now I'm what?"

Calvin looked Danielle in the eyes. "You're Danielle Tyler."

"And you're Calvin Chase."

They laid on the grass for the rest of the night trying to figure out who they were. Our sweet idiots, you were never going to figure that out. We decided who you would become. You two had some morals before prom, but we were happy they were gone. You thought you did worse things than backstabbing and manipulation. Your secrets were making you miserable, but the truths were going to be killing you. Have fun under the stars, because you weren't going to see them in your caskets once The Revenged Queen was done with you.

Chapter 15

"Well you didn't want to hang out with me tonight. I told you that I wanted to go out, and you said you had to finish up a project," Tucker said on the phone with Bethany.

Bethany was furious that Tucker was at Jordan's house with Emily. She didn't think she had any competition with Emily. She just knew she was bad news. "I thought you didn't like the girl because of Andrew."

"She's helping me with the Elizabeth situation."

"How?"

"She went through the same situation with Matt," he said.

She rolled her eyes. "She killed him, and I wished you saw that. I'll still love you, but I'm not supporting this friendship. I think it's foolish of you, if you ask me."

Tucker knew that Bethany could be controlling, but he was hoping she would come around. Well, she would become round, but that was for another reason. "Have fun with your project."

"Thank you," she said. She was too busy trying to fail a test at the moment. The only problem was, this test didn't exactly give her a chance to fail.

Bethany, we didn't know why you were so against it saying positive. We were perfectly fine that your new accessory would be a diaper bag.

"She's giving you a hard time," Emily said. She walked out on the balcony with a mixed drink for Tucker.

He took the cup and took a sip. He could tell it was strong, so he would take his time with it. He knew that he wouldn't become a lush, and we were proud of him for that. "She worries about me being at these parties. She's afraid that I'll have no one in my corner."

"You have me."

He looked at her. "She doubts it after everything with Andrew."

She nodded and took a seat. "Do you believe I caused him to go down the dark path again?" she asked.

"I think he did what he wanted. We all do stupid things. If we really look at it, we are the only two people that killed someone. Aren't we the true monsters of the world?"

"They were both accidents," Emily said.

"But that's not what the kids of Johnson Prep think." Tucker paused for a moment. "Elizabeth's son went to our school. I had no clue. He came up to me when the trial began. He recognized me instantly. I was underage, so my name was kept from public records. He exposed me to the world, and I couldn't do anything about it."

"What happened?"

"People started calling me Tucking Killer. I had a panic attack in the middle of the halls. People took photos and recorded the whole damn thing. People avoided me in the hallways." He looked down at his fingers. "I almost transferred."

"Why didn't you?"

"Because of Bethany. She defended me for so long against these people. She kept promising me that people would forget about it. They did when The Marked Queen came around at the beginning of the school year."

"Did she create her for that reason?" Emily asked. She knew she still needed to talk to Jordan about The Revenged Queen.

"I thought summer break would make people forget about it. We were the targets for the high society kids. We were done being the wallflowers, and we rose against it." And we wanted to thank you for the creation of The Marked Queen. You gave us everything we needed, and we couldn't have been happier about the turn of events.

Emily crossed her arms. "You ruined people's lives for what you did."

"Are you giving me a lecture?" he asked. He thought they understood each other. They wouldn't judge each other for everything they had done. "I thought we were trying to be friends."

She opened her mouth and shut it. "Have you gotten forgiveness from the family?"

"I got it from the husband. He knew that I was some innocent kid that made a mistake. I told my parents that I could drive home. They didn't know that I was drinking with my brother and sister in the other room at the summer party."

"Does your family hate you?"

He shook his head. "I wished they would. My siblings feel guilty for getting me that drunk. My parents were upset at first, but they chalked it up to me being youthful."

"It's good your family is so forgiving." She stood up. "I need a refill. I'll be right back," she said.

He stood up and leaned over the balcony. He took in a deep breath. "You really have people thinking you're so innocent, don't you?" Tucker heard a woman's voice say.

He turned and was startled. "You're dead." Elizabeth's brown hair was matted with her own blood. Her beautiful face was ruined by cuts from glass and skid marks from the road. Her blue dress was ripped and stained.

She smiled. "But guilt gave me a rebirth." She stood up. "You think you get to be a normal kid after everything you took from me? I didn't get to see my son graduate high school, I'll never grow old with my husband, and I'll never get to hold my future grandchildren."

"Your husband said you would have forgiven me," Tucker said. He could feel his heart racing. It must have been such a bitch to see that you didn't finish the job, Tucker. You were supposed to make sure they were dead, even in your guilt.

She laughed. "He was just trying to spare my feelings."

"Why can't you forgive me?"

She nodded. "Because you haven't told the truth of that night, have you?" she asked. He was quiet for a moment. "Exactly. I'm the only one that knows the truth. I know why it took so long for people to come to the scene." She stepped closer. She got close to his ear. "I know the reason why I couldn't be saved. Have fun sleeping with that tonight."

Tucker closed his eyes and opened them again. He looked around for Elizabeth, but she was gone. Tucker fell to the ground and began to breathe heavily. He tried his hardest to keep it together, but we all knew what it was like to be visited by a ghost from your past. Our only question was, what were you keeping from us, Tucker? Was she right? Was there more to the story? What did you do, Tucker?

Chapter 16

Jordan was laying in her bed after another successful party. She had kicked everyone else out and felt a high. She smiled, closing her eyes knowing that she kicked Danielle out of her party. She enjoyed watching Delilah standing up to Danielle, and she hoped to bring her down along with Bethany.

She felt someone sit on her bed. She assumed it was Val coming back from a party. "Val, can you stop playing with my hair. I'm trying to sleep."

"Who said it was Val?" Shane said.

Jordan looked up to see Shane sitting there. She was too drunk at the moment, and it startled her to see him there. "I thought I told everyone to leave."

"I know, but I thought I was special."

"I'm too drunk to do anything."

He laughed. He looked at his prey, and he was happy his newest victim actually was awake. He knew no one was home, so no one could stop them. He got on top of her. "But I thought you liked that I ignored the rumors."

Jordan tried to scream, but the alcohol took over. She tried to fight him, but she was too weak. "I don't want to have sex with you. Someone please help me! Get off of me!"

"But didn't The Marked Queen tell us that you wanted to make sure all your guest were satisfied? I'm not satisfied right now." He leaned down before she could protest. He crushed his lips on hers.

She felt bile rising in her throat. She felt his hands on her legs. He felt him begin to undress her. She squirmed, but she didn't have enough power. She didn't have enough strength.

The only thing that went through her mind was wishing it would stop and hating Bethany for leaking that rumor. This wouldn't be happening if it wasn't for her.

She felt his fingers go inside of her. "Don't be scared. You're going to enjoy this. Aren't you used to so many guys inside of you?" he laughed. He placed his hand on her mouth as she tried to scream. He began to kiss her body. She began to cry because she wanted the whole damn thing to stop. She wanted this all to be a nightmare.

"Get the fuck off of her!" Val screamed. She stormed into the room, grabbed Shane by his shirt, and pulled him off of Jordan. Jordan laid there motionless. She didn't know what to do.

"What the fuck?" Shane looked at Val. "She wanted this as much as I did."

"I doubt it from her crying, you psycho."

He got up and fixed her shirt. "Do you know the rumors about your sister? She loves being gang banged by everyone. She's a fucking slut."

"That doesn't give you the right to rape her!" Val wanted to kill this boy.

He smiled his evil grin. "Doesn't it? The Marked Queen was right about what she said about your sister." He paused. "Well, half right. I guess she only fucks athletes." He turned to walk out the door. "I've had better than her." He knew that he wouldn't face charges. He was rich and white. He could get away with murder in this country. He could thank Brock Turner for paving the path for him.

Val ignored him. She walked over to Jordan. "Are you okay?" she asked.

Jordan slid up in a sitting position. She had sobered up, not from his actions, but the words he spoke. She couldn't get the fact she was being shamed and raped was because of the blast form Bethany. "I just want a shower."

"Do you want to talk about it? We could go to the police," Val said.

Jordan turned to Val. She laughed in her face. "You seriously are so naïve. You think anything is going to happen to him? It's my word against his, and mine means nothing." She stood up. "He was right, I'm just a damn slut, and I deserved this."

She grabbed Jordan by the face. "No one deserves what just happened to you. You might think you don't matter, but you do."

"Val, I never once said I didn't matter. What pisses me off is this fucking rumor against me? I continue to get bashed for having consensual sex. People want to call me a slut and think they can come into my damn house and take advantage of me!" she screamed. "Fuck anyone who thinks that I deserve any of this bullshit." Jordan stormed out of the room.

She walked into the bathroom and started a shower. She took off her clothes. She saw the bruises from Shane's grip on her. She felt like her body didn't belong to her. She felt like she was now a stranger, and she didn't know how to feel normal. She took comfort in the warm water. She washed herself clean in the water, but it didn't make her forget what just happened.

She got out of the shower and toweled herself off. She wiped the steam from the mirror as she pulled her hair behind her ear. She wouldn't let this moment ruin her. This incident would fire her soul. "I will destroy you, bitch," Jordan said, with so much anger in her voice. Bethany caused all of this, and she would pay for everything she did. "I'm The Revenged Queen, and you're going to find out what that fully fucking means." Jordan walked out of the bathroom leaving the sexual assault feelings in the room behind her.

Chapter 17

"You seem off today," Delilah said, looking at Jordan.

Jordan smiled. "I'm a little hungover from the party last night." Jordan tried to walk past Delilah.

Delilah saw the bruises on Jordan's arms. "What are those from?"

Jordan didn't need a friend to worry about her right now. She wanted to forget about the whole damn thing. "I fell down the stairs."

"Are you okay?" Delilah asked. She thought maybe they should have this meeting for another day. She wanted to make sure Jordan was okay.

Delilah, a day off wasn't going to make Jordan feel better. She was going to live with the scars from last night for a long time. She needed to focus on taking down the person that caused it all.

"If I wasn't, then I wouldn't be here. Delilah, we are trying to take down Bethany. We don't have time to worry about fucking bruises that will fade away." Jordan knew they were on a time crunch. Graduation was in two weeks. They needed to make sure everything went down flawlessly.

They walked into the computer lab to see Carter sitting behind a computer. He looked up to see Jordan and Delilah walk in. Carter got up. "I thought this was between us," Carter said.

Jordan rolled her eyes. "Please, she wants revenge on the bitch as much as we do." Jordan walked over and took a seat on the table. "What dirt do you have on us?"

Delilah looked at Carter. She was surprised that he was actually here for this. "Why are you helping us?" she asked.

"Because of what Bethany did to Jasmine."

Jordan rolled her eyes. "Yeah, the fat bitch actually has a boyfriend."

Carter glared at Jordan. He was tired of people calling Jasmine fat. Carter, we got that you thought she was beautiful and skinny. It made us want to barf, but you needed to realize love made you blind. She might have looked skinny with that tan, but she wasn't fooling anyone. "She's not fat. I won't help you, if you continue to bash her."

Delilah walked up to him. She pulled out money from her purse. "I want you to get dirt on Danielle." What is with these girls throwing cash at the hacker? Maybe he should have gotten into this business a long time ago. It wasn't like he spent his weekend getting test answers for other kids at other schools. Oh wait. It was why he looked down on everyone? The rich loved a shortcut, and he loved getting paid.

Jordan laughed. "Don't worry, Delilah. I didn't forget about you. I made sure to give him extra to find dirt on Danielle and Calvin."

"I thought our main focus today should be Bethany."

"What did you find out?" Jordan asked. She also gave Carter the information her private investigator found out about Bethany too.

"Not much. She has an appointment tomorrow with her OBGYN. She also has been seeing her grades slip," Carter said, showing them the proof.

Jordan was disappointed. "This bitch would be squeaky clean."

Jordan, you weren't trying hard enough. We knew you were new to the bitch game, but you had to work at this. It wasn't like a cock that was presented to you.

"I wouldn't say that." Carter turned to her. "She's about to fail her classes, and her OBGYN also performs abortions."

"There's no way Bethany's knocked up," Delilah said. She knew Bethany might have been a bitch, but she couldn't see her and Tucker fucking.

Jordan crossed her arms. "Delilah's right. The grade angle is a good one, but she needs to cheat or something. She's dumb as rocks. It doesn't really help us out," Jordan paused. "But I can put a fire under her ass. Jordan pulled out her second phone. She bought it for this occasion.

Bethany, you were becoming quite an interesting story. You built a persona on beauty and brains. I knew you didn't have the beauty, because why would you be with the mouth breather? It was okay that you thought so low of yourself. We get with your looks you have to have some delusion. Maybe you put too much on your plate trying to take the kingdom from Danielle. D's don't look good on you Ms. Valedictorian. -The Revenged Queen.

Jordan leaned forward and took a photo of her history grade. She then pressed the sent button. "There."

"What does that accomplish?" Carter asked.

"She's going to eventually come to you. She knows her grades are going to suffer. She builds herself on being the best. She's going to get you to hack the school records to get you to change her grades."

"How will she know to go to him?" Delilah asked.

Jordan laughed. "How do you think I found him? It's called your reputation." Jordan grabbed her purse. "She wants to believe that I'm just some dumb slut, well at least I can keep my grades up the proper way."

"You really have thought of this all," Carter said.

"She deserves to pay for everything she's fucking done. Don't you see all three of us have been burned by that bitch? She said it was time all of us pay for our actions, well I believe the same for her. It's time for her day in court." She turned to Carter. "Keep me posted." Jordan stormed out of the room because she knew she was working herself up. She had a flashback to last night, and she wanted to forget about it.

Delilah smiled. "I guess you're part of The Revenged Queen family."

"I'll do whatever I need to take Bethany down, but I won't stoop to her level."

Delilah nodded. "We won't either."

"I'm not so sure. Revenge can make you worse."

Delilah chuckled. "They did this to themselves." Delilah turned and walked out of the room.

Carter sat down at the computer screen. He clicked on another file. It was an appointment book. It had Bethany's name marked to be schedule for an abortion the next day. HIPPA was useless when people could hack their way to the dirty little secrets.

Bethany, you thought you were untouchable, but you had a secret attack coming your way. You believed you could have this moment in private, but the school would soon find out. Hoped you had a great Valedictorian speech because no one would remember it once Jordan gave her's.

Zachary Ryan

****

"Are you sure you want to do this?" the nurse asked Bethany.

Bethany wanted to be truthful with the nurse. She wanted to admit that she didn't even want to have this surgery. She wished she had the strength to carry this child to full term. She knew there would be stigmas, but she knew it wasn't her time to have a child.

Bethany closed her eyes. "Yes, I'm sure."

The nurse nodded. "Okay. We need to prep you then."

The nurse made Bethany change out of her clothes. She made Bethany lie down. "I'm going to give you some medicine to make you fall asleep. We will give you anesthesia before we start the procedure. This is to calm you," the nurse explained.

Bethany closed her eyes, trying to forget about what was about to happen. She was doing this alone, and she wished she could have told someone. She prayed no one would judge her for making this choice. She was doing what she thought would get her ahead. She took in a deep breath and let the drugs take over.

****

Bethany was holding her three-month son. "You're so beautiful," she said. He had Tucker's beautiful eyes.

Tucker walked into their cabin. He looked frantic. "We need to pack up quickly."

Bethany looked at him with worry. "Why's that?" she asked.

"Bethany, they're coming for you."

"What?" Bethany had no clue why people were trying to attack her. She has done nothing wrong. They lived in a cabin in the middle of nowhere. She was a no one.

Bethany, we thought this was the perfect place for you, bitch.

There was commotion outside. Tucker looked outside. "It's too late. They're here for you."

Bethany grabbed Grayson. "No one is going to separate us."

The door opened. "I doubt that." It was a woman wearing all black. Bethany tried to figure out who she was, but the problem was, she couldn't see who she was thanks to the mask she wore over her face.

"We haven't done anything to you!" Bethany screamed.

People ambushed the small cabin. They grabbed Bethany, Tucker, and Grayson. Bethany tried to fight, but the grip was too tight on her. She was dragged outside. She saw two stakes. Tucker and Bethany were tied to each one. People began to put wood around them.

"Are you seriously about to burn us?" Bethany asked. She turned to Tucker. "What did we do?"

"You exposed the high court," the masked woman said. "You have ruined our kingdom, and you've made it easy for people to attack. You thought you were above the rules of our land, and you must now pay the consequences."

"I never said anything." Bethany had no clue what this woman was saying. She wanted to know where all of this was coming from.

"Don't lie!" People started screaming at Bethany. The servants began to put lighter fluid on the wood.

The masked woman grabbed a torch and light it. Bethany turned to Tucker. "I love you so much."

Tucker smiled. "We did it for Grayson." He turned to look at the people. "We exposed you because you all deserved it. You tried to ruin our lives over and over again. We won't be ashamed for what we did." Tucker knew that this could happen. He wanted them all to feel ashamed for what they have truly done to this land.

The masked woman laughed. "You really think you could change the hierarchy of this land? You don't get it. We will always rule, and you'll still be the peasants. It's how the natural order works."

Grayson began to cry. "Give me back my baby." Bethany tried to fight her ropes, but they kept her in place.

The masked woman took Grayson from one of her servants hands. "You knew the sacrifice you were making. You can stop with the innocent card. You knew what would happen if you were caught. You started this all on your own. You get to die watching me take your baby away from you."

"Give me back my son!" Bethany screamed.

"Your sentence has been decided." The masked woman turned to the man with another torch. She signaled for Tucker's burning. The man lit the wood under Tucker's feet. He began to scream when the flames consumed him.

"TUCKER!" Bethany screamed, and began to cry. She felt completely defeated in that moment. He was the only man to truly love her, and she had just watched him burn to a crisp. She shook her head. "He was innocent. He didn't do anything," she said.

"He was still your accomplice. It's your fault he's dead." She walked toward Bethany with the torch.

"Who are you?" Bethany asked of this masked figure.

The woman smiled. "I'm The Revenged Queen. I was created because of you. Have fun knowing you caused your own downfall. Isn't that a bitch?" The Revenged Queen then lit Bethany's wood on fire. Bethany screamed until she woke up from her dream.

She was confused and delirious. "Bethany, it's going to be okay. Your procedure went perfectly. You're going to feel some discomfort for some time. We just need you to relax in the bed until the medication wears off. Do you understand?" the nurse asked.

Bethany looked at her. She felt the tears fall down her face. She grabbed her stomach, and her son was no longer in her stomach. She nodded, because she was too emotional to speak. Bethany remembered the dream, and she didn't want to believe that she created her downfall. She called them out on their bullshit. She didn't cause any harm to anyone. Why couldn't people see that?

You were native till the end. We hoped that dream came true for you, The Marked Queen. We gave you sympathy for what you just went through, but we all knew you only did it so no one could have dirt on you. The only problem was, people would find out about this soon enough, and we wondered if you still thought it was worth it in the end? It was time for you to be tried and we loved the idea of you burning at the stake, bitch.

Chapter 18

"I'm sorry that I have to cut this short," Danielle said with a wink. Christian thought it would be a good idea if she went into the one-on-one sessions of the website. She was told she would make a lot more money, and she was a desperate whore for the green.

"Can't I have just another ten minutes?" the older gentleman asked.

"Sorry, you know the rules." Danielle paused. "I'll be back on tomorrow." She turned and slipped the one bra strap. "Maybe I'll take off both next time." She looked back to see the guy nearly die from how big his boner was.

"I'm looking forward to it."

Danielle laughed as she logged off. She closed her laptop and turned to see Dan standing there. God, why did this guy have to be such a buzz kill? She grabbed her robe. "Dan, what are you doing here?"

"I wanted to see how you were doing. I hadn't heard from you in a couple of days. What the fuck are you doing?" Dan hadn't expected to walk in on his girlfriend basically strip teasing. "Are you cheating on me?"

We wished. We were over your moral high grounds. We wanted our bitch back, and she couldn't with you around.

She walked over to him. She kissed him on the cheek. "I'm not cheating on you. I've been doing webcam videos for a little over a week now."

"Why?" he asked.

"We needed the cash. My mom wasn't making enough at the diner. Christian suggested the website to me, and I've been making daily web videos. Christian got me into the one-on-one just yesterday."

"Are you kidding me right now?"

"What?"

"Can't you just be normal for once? Can't you have a job, and there be no scandal involved?"

Dan, we were over how stupid you were. This was Johnson Prep, there was no such thing as no scandal.

Danielle crossed her arms. "You knew what you were getting into."

"I met a good girl on the swing set." He ran his fingers through his hair. "I thought we were done with this bullshit. I thought you were going to have a moral high ground."

"You sound like my mother. There's no such thing as a moral high ground when you're fucking desperate." She shook her head. "You think I want to be showing off my body for perverts? I'd rather be showing it only to you."

"Why don't you stop?"

"We need the money. I can't afford college alone anymore. I gave up my dad's money, so I could be the person you wanted me to be."

"So, now it's my fault you're taking off your clothes like a whore?"

She shrugged. He did cause you to realize how horrible you were when you had daddy's money. We preferred you that way, but we were enjoying the desperate Danielle too. "I don't see anything wrong with this. I'm not hurting anyone or losing myself in it."

"It's still horrible to do. It's not normal."

Danielle looked at Dan, and she was done with him. She cried a couple weeks ago about how much she couldn't be

Zachary Ryan

without him. She realized that he didn't fit in her world. She knew that these were controversial ideas, but she needed to make the money. She was tired of having someone judge every fucking move she makes. "Fuck you, Dan."

"What?"

She walked straight up to him and slapped him across the face. "Fuck you. I'm done with your judgmental ass."

"It's called integrity."

"It must be a nice concept to have when you aren't fearing the fact that you might be living on the streets. You've always wanted me to be this version of myself that never works out. I was a bitch on my dad's money, and now I'm a whore on perverts' money. I'll never be what you want."

"I just want the best for you," Dan said.

He didn't want this to be the end, but we were over you. Danielle said it right. You were nothing more than a judgmental prick. We get that you love a boring life, but we didn't want our fallen queen to be one.

"Guess what? This is what's best for me. We are catching up on late bills. I can start saving for college. I'm building a future for myself. Instead of you being proud of me, you're here to tear me down."

"Does your mother know what you do?"

Danielle shrugged. "Tell her because I don't care anymore." She got into his face. "I get enough bullshit from the girls at school. I don't need it from my man." She pushed him toward the door.

"Are you ending it with me?" he asked.

Danielle looked at him. She wanted to feel sadness for those puppy dog eyes, but she would rather barf at the moment. "I guess you could say I had a lapse of judgment pleading for you

86

to take me back. Have fun with your normal life. I'll be dancing in the shadows." She slammed the door in his face.

Well done, Danielle. We never thought you had it in you. We assumed Dan would be around until the bitter end, but it was refreshing to see the trash has finally been taken out. You knew what you were doing. You were providing for your family, and we had to commend you on that. We truly wanted to be proud of you for the fact that you were about to give your best friend the knife to finally stab you in the back this time. Hoped you liked taking your clothes off for men, because after The Revenged Queen was done with you, we had a feeling that was the only job you would ever get.

Chapter 19

Our sweet Calvin, what did we tell you about looking at your ex's photos with their new beard? Calvin tried to ignore the pain of seeing Aman happily in love with Sana. He knew they could never post photos of them together, but he had so many saved on his phone. He wondered if they would ever get back to those moments together.

He sighed. He grabbed his drink and started to down it. He wanted to forget about it, and he hoped being at a gay bar would help him. He was awkwardly in the corner ignoring everyone, as people were dancing to the music.

"You know it's not good to be standing alone at a bar," a guy said, coming up to Calvin.

Calvin looked at him. He looked a lot like Aman. He had dark features, a nice smile, brown skin, and he had his black hair slicked back. Calvin's heart ached for a second. Calvin finished his drink. "I guess I'm not used to the club scene."

The guy raised an eyebrow. "Are you telling me that you really don't come out often?"

"Newly single."

"That makes sense why I haven't seen you on any of the hook up apps."

Calvin laughed. He forgot that was another way to get someone to come home with him. Calvin, were you telling us that you were planning on being a gay whore? We told you the gay world was way more bitchier and sluttier than the straight one. "I guess I don't really see the need of them."

"Because guys come up to you all the time in a club?" The guy signaled the bartender to bring them some shots.

"Do you come here often?" Calvin asked.

"Is that your pick-up line?" The guy even raised his eyebrow like Aman.

Calvin blushed. "You can tell I'm out of the game."

The guy smiled, and Calvin felt safe in that smile. He also thought of Terrell. He thought Terrell would be his entrance into the gay world, and he didn't want to be naïve again. He would keep up his guard, and he would make sure no one used him again. "I'm Omar by the way." He put out his hand.

"Cavin," Calvin said, as he shook his hand. Aw, they made introductions. Hopefully they got to know each other with their mouths. We wanted some gay hook up sessions, not a romance. We had enough of him being in love in the first book.

The shots came, and they took them. Omar asked if Calvin wanted to dance, and he didn't see why there was a problem. They were on the dance floor enjoying life. Calvin closed his eyes, and he let freedom take over. He finally felt like he was grasping at the reality of being gay in New York City.

He looked at Omar, who looked cute with the strobe lights dancing off his face. He felt aroused in this moment. He thought back to his conversation with Danielle. She believed that he could find love in this world, but he wasn't so sure. Terrell was so unapologetic about using him for sex. He hasn't heard from Terrell since that day. He thought of Aman in that moment too. He felt like his dirty skeleton in the closet.

Calvin knew love wasn't in his cards, and that was okay. He would sleep his way through the city then. He would have great stories, and he would lock his heart up. We enjoyed your knew open-asshole, closed-heart policy. Calvin, we applauded you for your new epiphany of being our bottom slut.

Calvin grabbed Omar's shirt and pulled him in for a kiss. They began to make out on the dance floor. Calvin grabbed

Omar's ass, and he enjoyed how thick his ass and thighs were. He felt Omar's lips on his neck and the tinge of sensation when Omar bit down.

Their boners were ready to be freed, and they needed a quiet place to go. Omar suggested the bathroom, because nothing said sexy like a dingy, cum-stained bathroom stall. They walked into the bathroom and went to the handicap stalls.

Omar pushed Calvin against the wall and began exploring his body. Calvin ran his fingers in Omar's hair and grabbed on when Omar unzipped Calvin's pants. Omar got down on his knees and began pleasuring Calvin. Calvin never got this much enjoyment from any of the guys he has been with before. Calvin, this was what happened when you stopped trying to have a fairytale.

"I'm so close," Calvin said about to release.

"You must have not had sex for a while." Omar stopped blowing him. "I don't want you to unload until I get to put it in your tight ass." Omar flipped him over.

Calvin felt the cool tile on his skin. He heard Omar's pants fall to the ground. He took in a sharp breath when he felt Omar's fingers go inside of him. He moaned and craved more of Omar. He didn't feel taken advantage of this time. He felt desired.

They weren't quiet when Omar began to thrust. They weren't shy about how much pleasure they were getting from this. Calvin, you were the innocent boy looking for romance, and now you were a cock thirsty girl in a dirty bathroom.

Omar bit down on Calvin's neck when he climaxed, and they both screamed once it was all said and done. They received a round of applause once they were done. Aw, you two thought you had the bathroom to yourselves. No one would tell on you boys because they were doing the same thing.

Calvin turned around and looked in Omar's eyes. "That was incredible," Calvin said.

Omar smirked. He leaned forward and kissed him on the lips. "You do know your way around small spaces." He got up close to his ear. "I wonder how you would do in my bedroom," he whispered.

Calvin would have liked that, but he knew to keep it a one-night stand right now. He couldn't afford the excitement of the future. Calvin pushed Omar back. "This was all great, but I can't right now. He pulled up his pants. "I wish I could do round two with you, but it's not going to happen." Calvin opened the bathroom stall.

"What the fuck?" Omar said.

Calvin ran out of the bathroom and the club. He wished he wasn't so damaged, and he could have gotten to know Omar. He wished he could believe that there would be something more than a bathroom fuck session. Calvin, you did the right thing, because it would have been embarrassing assuming you would have more with the hot Indian. Calvin, you should be proud of being the new slut in school, but how would you feel once things went downhill, and The Revenged Queen found out? You had better enjoy your little fuck session behind closed doors, because everyone was about to find out how used up your asshole was.

Zachary Ryan

Chapter 20

"Can we talk about the other night?" Val asked, walking into Jordan's room.

Jordan looked up at her sister. She saw the concern in her eyes, and she wanted to forget about the incident with Shane. "Val, I'm in the middle of something." Jordan wanted to spend her energy finding a way to destroy everyone involved with The Marked Queen.

Val walked over and took a seat on Jordan's bed. "I don't like the idea of you just shutting down because of what happened."

Jordan closed her laptop. She was tired of looking at Bethany's ugly face. Jordan, that was mean. Sure, she wasn't the prettiest girl, or the sexiest, or even spank bank material, but she still had some looks, right? "I was sexually assaulted. I'm the one that gets to decide how we move forward."

"But you're not talking about it."

"Because I'm at fault for it." Jordan looked Val in the eyes.

"What?" Val seemed confused. "How are you at fault?"

"Bethany was right. Shane was right. Everyone in that fucking school was right. I'm the giant slut everyone knows me for. I had sex with both the football team and the lacrosse team. Shit, I would have sex with anyone. It was my reputation, and I didn't care."

"That doesn't mean people can take advantage of you."

"Doesn't it? Our parents are never home to give me love. You're only home for break. Val, I'm alone in this house. If Bethany never posted that about me, then I would have let Shane sleep with me." Jordan got off her bed.

92

Val grabbed her. "But she did. You realized you didn't want to be the easy girl anymore."

"I invited him here to have sex with him. That was the point of him being here. A part of me caused it." Jordan shook her head. "This is so stupid. I'm the party girl. I don't get to have feelings or be in a relationship. I'm here to please my guests."

Val got up and pulled Jordan into a hug. She wanted Jordan to feel like she has someone in her corner. She knew her parents weren't ever around. They were too busy living their lives. It wasn't their fault they never wanted kids, and they thought being rich made them immune from unwanted pregnancies.

"What do you want?" Val asked.

"I want someone I can count on." She knew she had Emily, but she was going through her own shit. She liked that Emily had Tucker, but she thought of him as a band aid. Emily wasn't over what happened with Matthew.

"You have me."

"For now, I have another year of high school. I have another year of these fake assholes, and I want nothing to do with them. Why can't I meet someone that won't look at me for a good time?" Jordan raised her hands in the air. "I know damn well that's why half these assholes are friends with me. I'm the good time. I failed Shane because I rejected him. I didn't live up to my persona."

Val didn't say anything at first. She couldn't believe Jordan was putting the blame on herself. "Jordan," she said, with a weak voice.

Jordan laughed. "This is why I didn't want to have this conversation. Val, I love you. You've been away for a while now. You might as well act like you aren't here. I don't need a big sister, because we all know it's bullshit." Jordan walked out of the room and to the bathroom. She closed the door and turned on the shower and laid on the floor. She wrapped her arms around her knees and cried. She never could get the disgust of Shane off her body. She wanted to believe she had control of her life, but it was never going to happen. She clung to The Revenged Queen, praying that this would give her the power back. This queen was a sad, lonely girl who always threw the lavish parties, but no one ever stayed to clean up with her.

Chapter 21

"Del, I'm so sorry that I missed our date for tonight," Matt said, walking into the living room.

Delilah and her father had planned to see another author together. She closed the latest book by Edgar Mitchell. It was the author she was planning to hear from tonight. She stood up. "It's fine. I shouldn't be surprised. You're an accomplished author. It's the name of the game."

"Let me make it up to you," he said.

She laughed. "Like the birthdays, dances, and any other high school accomplishment of mine?"

"Where is this coming from?" he asked. He had never seen her with so much anger in his daughter before.

She took a seat on the edge of the couch across from her father. "Maybe because I'm done having a father only around a couple of times a month. I'm about to graduate high school in two weeks. Are you even going to be there?" she asked. She needed her dad more than ever with her mother giving her the cold shoulder. Her brother, Ethan, continued to ignore her calls because he was in the middle of finals.

"You knew this was the name of the game. You're going to be traveling a lot when your book comes out."

"What book?" She paused. "Do you even know what's going on in my life?"

"You turned in your essay for the scholarship. You're getting your grades up." Matt had been so busy promoting his new book, having different panels, and going to film sets that he hasn't had time to check on his daughter.

"And sleeping with my principal."

"What?"

"Didn't mommy dearest tell you?"

He fixed his glasses. "Your mother never mentioned it to me. I figured she would tell me about such a bomb."

"Or a father would know what's going on in their daughter's life." She stood up again. "I get it. I'm not one of your millions of fans." Delilah thought her father would come running when he found out about her scandal with the principal. She wanted nothing more than for her father to be around, but she was an idiot to believe otherwise. Aw Delilah, you thought your father cared about you opening your legs for older men. He was accomplishing his goals and not worried about you polishing off a cock.

"You're my daughter. I'll always be here for you," Matt said, even if he wasn't sure of it himself. Matt, you have got to do a better job of disciplining her. Maybe a light spanking, although she might moan and call you daddy.

"That's a load of shit. You would think as a writer, you would come up with a better speech."

"Where's this attitude coming from? Is it from Danielle? I never cared for her."

"If you were around, you would know she and I aren't friends."

"What did she do?"

"How do you think it got out I was banging the principle?" Delilah rolled her eyes. "I get you think you're the father of the year, but it's all bullshit. Look at New York City. Look at the kids at Johnson Prep."

"What do you mean?" he asked.

Delilah had a moment of clarity. We didn't think the dumb bitch could have any of those. We were proud of the new

Delilah. You were surprising us every day. "Our parents are jokes. We are left unsupervised and look how we turn out. Everyone is backstabbing each other, sleeping with each other, and drugs are our actual extracurricular."

"Every writer needs to have some wild moments in their lives."

Delilah was frustrated with her father in that moment. "Stop talking to me like I'm a fucking writer. Talk to me like I'm your daughter. Do you even care that I banged my principal?"

"You're eighteen. I don't have a say on your life anymore."

She clapped. "That's the best response I'm going to get from you." She shook her head.

"What else do you want me to do?"

"Scream or ground me. Do something that a normal father would do?"

"Now who is being naïve? Del, I'm not a normal father. Your mother isn't a normal mother. We have a life in front of the spotlight. We have fans wanting our autographs, we have publishers demanding us to pump out new novels, and we have ourselves clinging to stay in the spotlight."

"And that has to affect me?" she asked.

"You wanted this life." He paused. "Ethan didn't have any complaints with it."

Delilah rolled her eyes. "Ethan spent most of his time playing lacrosse, smoking weed, and jacking off. You really think he gave two shits if his parents were involved in his life?"

"And you've spent your time writing, finding yourself, and blaming us for everything wrong in your life."

"Isn't it?"

Matt knew he made his fair share of mistakes. "I have always been here for you growing up. Yes, I've missed things, but I did them as you got older. You were strong and independent."

"But you never being around made me feel worthless and forgotten."

"And you were supposed to get it out in your writing." He grabbed his briefcase. "I'm disappointed that you slept with your principal, but you're an adult. I'm supposed to raise you until eighteen and let you go. This is all about your own choices," he said. He turned and walked away.

Delilah was left stunned that her father would be so cold to her. He was encouraging her to be confident in her writing only a couple of weeks ago. Delilah, you shouldn't make it hard on yourself. Your father's new book just tanked, and he wasn't too pleased. He was right though, you were an adult, so your choices in the next couple of weeks were all yours. We hoped you could still be daddy's little girl once you were done tarnishing him and your mother's name.

Chapter 22

"You had an abortion?" Tucker asked, looking at Bethany.

Bethany, we assumed you would have told him in a more subtle way.

"Yes," she said. She still felt some discomfort from the procedure. She couldn't shake the dream she had. We didn't want you to worry too much. That dream would come true sooner than you thought.

"Why am I finding out now?" Tucker was furious. They had always been a team, and he felt like this was the type of news he should have known sooner.

She rolled her eyes. "You aren't strong enough to deal with something like this. I had to do it for the sake of the both of us."

He nodded. "Really? You think that I'm that weak?"

She leaned forward into his bubble. "You're hanging out with Emily for some therapeutic bullshit. You can't tell me you haven't fallen off the wagon a little. You're so desperate to connect with someone."

"And you're such a bitch since it came out that you're The Marked Queen, that you can't realize how horrible you've been." Tucker stood up off her bed. "Are you seriously not upset about this?"

"It had to be done."

"We could have raised this baby together," Tucker said. He had always wanted kids. He thought it would have happened later in life, but he would have been a father to that child.

She remembered her dream. "So we could be destroyed by our peers? We finally have control of the school."

"What control?" Tucker asked. He threw his hands in the air. "We graduate in two weeks. We did what we needed to. You told me once we started all of this, it would be done by prom."

Sweet Tucker, she planned on it being done by prom, but she relished in the power. She didn't want it to go away.

"We aren't the wallflowers anymore. People look at us in the hallways. Can't you see how glorious it's been?"

"What I see is a girl that's lost her way, a guy trying to find peace after a note he got about a car accident, and another girl trying to find true friends. The Marked Queen's glory is over. We're all fucked up after it." Tucker could tell how lonely and scared Susan was. He tried to connect with her, but he was dealing with his own demons.

"So, you regret what we did?" Bethany asked.

Bethany, we knew you had no regrets in taking down the high court, but your minions are the ones paying the price.

Tucker pulled out a piece of paper. He slammed it in Bethany's chest. It was the note he got from The Revenged Queen. "We're now targeted. I'm about to relive everything that happened last year. We did this so people would forget."

Bethany read the note. "She's just bluffing. If she was coming after us, she would have by now. I think it's some low life trying to scare us."

He nodded. "That's what people thought of us in the beginning." He paused. "That's why you had the abortion. You wanted to make preemptive measures just in case."

Bethany kept her mouth shut. She didn't owe him an explanation. Actually, she did since it was his child, after all. Shouldn't you have given him some clarity? "I'm not going to ruin my future or yours for a mistake that happened."

"You were the one to say we shouldn't use a condom. You didn't want people to know that you're freakier in the bedroom." We didn't need to know the bitch liked pearl necklaces, and we weren't talking about jewelry.

"Tucker, you don't get to judge me," she said.

"I can damn well do what I want," he said.

"I didn't kill a person from a car accident."

He shouldn't have been surprised that his girlfriend would go below the belt. She didn't like being backed into a corner, and he wasn't going to back down. "Some people would think you murdered a baby." He paused. "I guess we both have killer instincts." You two did make a delicious couple. We just chalked you both up to being boring bible thumpers, but you guys were far more entertaining than the rich bitches.

"I'm graduating top of our class. I'll be going off to Brown in the fall. You will not make me feel guilty for keeping that intact."

"But you never communicated with me. I would have agreed to an abortion, because we are too young for kids right now. You just assumed I couldn't take care of it. I wasn't strong enough in your eyes to deal with a blow like this." He grabbed his camera bag.

She crossed her arms. "Are you ending it with me?" she asked.

"I'm too much in love with you to do that, but I'm not enjoying what I see."

She laughed. "And you're a misogynistic asshole to think I'm going to change who I am because of a hurt man's feelings."

"I would never make you change, but you should be a better person. I need to get out of here." He left the room, and he left the future of their relationship right there.

Bethany watched him walk out of that room, and she wasn't upset. She wasn't going to let anyone bring her down. She was The Marked Queen, and that was all that mattered right now. Bethany, you kept sitting at your throne as your subjects walked away from your castle. You were making it too easy for The Revenged Queen to take over your spot.

****

Emily was smoking outside on Jordan's balcony. She hadn't seen much of her since her party, but she knew one thing she needed to bring up to her. Jordan walked out, surprised to see Emily smoking. "When did you pick up smoking?" she asked.

Emily turned and smiled. "Since I'm sending boys to heaven and rehab, I thought smoking would be a nice touch to the image."

Jordan laughed. "You're so weird." She stood next to her. She took the cigarette out of her hand and took a puff. She turned to see Emily giving her a weird look. "I'm the party girl slut. It's in my nature to want a cigarette."

Emily was the one to laugh this time. "I guess we are really killing it at this reputation game."

"The seniors made a name for us, so what ever shall we do?"

"It seems you're the one terrorizing the seniors, or trying to," Emily said, remembering Tucker's note.

"What are you talking about?" Jordan asked. She had to play innocent. She knew Emily was loyal, but she was a dark horse. She didn't know if she wanted Emily in The Revenged Queen fold.

Emily turned to look at Jordan. "I'm not a fucking idiot. I know you're The Revenged Queen."

"Who is that?"

Emily rolled her eyes. "I saw the note you sent Tucker. Bitch, I've been best friends with you for years. I know your damn handwriting."

Jordan knew she was busted, and she couldn't play it off anymore. "I should have typed the stupid thing."

"It makes it more personal if you handwrite it." Emily paused.

Jordan pushed Emily. "You're so fucking stupid."

"I do what I can. So… why?"

Jordan could tell Emily about the rape. She could tell Emily about how much she hated her life being put on blast. She could tell her how she needed something to distract her from the sheer quietness in the house she lived in. "I didn't want Bethany to get the satisfaction of having something on all of us," Jordan said.

"The blast she said about you." Emily hadn't really paid attention to The Marked Queen drama. She already dealt with being the girl that murdered Matthew Ryan her freshman year. People tended to leave her alone. They didn't know if she would kill them next.

"I'm not ashamed of sleeping around. I shouldn't be bashed for it."

"Bitch, you were fucking basically all the athletes."

Jordan felt a little hurt by Emily's words. She never thought her best friend would think of her as a slut. "Like you needed to be called out for being a killer."

Emily felt her anger start to course through her. "You know damn well I didn't kill him."

"And I'm not a slut. I'm not someone that you can easily fuck and think it's alright. I'm not some slam piece that doesn't have feelings or wants anything real," Jordan said, and she felt good getting it off her chest.

Emily could tell that Jordan's parents never being around affected her. She pulled Jordan in for a hug. "You always have me. I'm not going anywhere."

"But you have Tucker now, which is weird." Jordan didn't like Emily hanging out with him. She wanted to know where her loyalty stood.

"I'm hanging out with him because he understands what I'm going through."\

"But if it gets out that I'm the Revenged Queen," Jordan said.

Emily looked her straight in the eyes. "Then I'll choose your crazy ass."

"How did you move forward after Matthew?" Jordan asked.

"I didn't. I'm still trying to process everything. I keep attracting these lost souls, and I'm too weak to help them out."

"Are you trying to help Tucker?"

She shrugged. "I don't know. We both found comfort with each other, and it's nice." She looked away from Jordan. She looked at the city lights. "It doesn't mean that I forget everything with Matthew. It doesn't mean I stopped loving him," Emily said.

Jordan pulled Emily in close. It was refreshing seeing these juniors bonding together. These two would never betray each other, because life has already done that for them. "I believe you'll never stop loving Matthew, but you need to move forward with your life. You can't cling to him. Maybe Tucker could be someone for you."

"But he's with Bethany."

"I don't see that lasting. And wouldn't it be so fun to see him dump her for you."

Emily looked at Jordan. "You really want to take the bitch down?"

"More than anything. She believed that she could call us out on our shit with no consequences. I think it's time she paid."

Emily nodded. "I'll help you any way you need me to."

"I don't want you to help out, if you're not strong enough."

"She hurt my best friend, and I want to make sure she gets what she deserves."

"That's my girl," Jordan said, hugging her tighter. It looked like there was a new addition into The Revenged Queen family. We hoped Emily didn't let her past demons sway her from helping Jordan achieve her goal. We just are missing one more bitch to join the squad. Our only question was, who would be the last person to want to get revenge on The Marked Queen herself? Boys and girls, it was about to get interesting as the seniors put on their cap and gowns. It was time to send them off with a bang.

Chapter 23

Delilah was wearing her most proper dress: a short, backless black dress with long sleeves. She had her hair pulled into a bun. She was trying to look elegant, while drinking a martini. Delilah, there was nothing elegant about your ass.

"Is this seat taken?" a gentleman asked. He was in his mid to late forties, with salt and pepper hair. He seemed fit under his suit, and he had bright blue eyes you wanted to swim in.

Delilah turned and smiled. "Of course." She tried to have a twinkle in her eye. Delilah, you most certainly had a type.

"What is a pretty girl like you doing in a place like this alone?" he asked.

She shrugged. "Sometimes you need to get away from your life. I couldn't stay at home anymore." Is that because your dad wasn't there, and it reminded you how much he really didn't care for you?

"Troubles in paradise?"

She laughed and touched his arm. "I just don't really know people in my life. You think they care for you, but they just turn out to be imposters."

"Boyfriend troubles?" he asked. If you had only known what troubles she had. They could be summed with one word: daddy.

"No, I'm very single." She waved him off. "Let's not talk about my troubles." She turned to face him. "I want to get to know you more."

He smiled, and he had a beautiful smile. Delilah knew how to catch herself a winner. Well, we didn't know if Principal Grand was a winner, but we could only assumed he was good in bed. It was why she went back to him during her meltdown. Well, she might still be going through it right now.

"I'm Richard." He put out his hand.

"Delilah," she said, shaking his hand.

"That's a pretty name for a pretty girl."

She leaned forward. "You should see me out of these clothes." She winked and took a sip of her martini. Delilah, you were such a little minx. We applauded this side of you. How could we not enjoy your newfound confidence?

He signaled for a drink for him and her. He placed a hand on her thigh. "I wouldn't mind taking you home tonight. I hope you don't have work early in the morning."

She turned to give him her profile. "I can move some things around." You mean, what periods you were planning to skip. You were a senior after all, you didn't really have to be there. It must have been hard being a high school student. Hoped he didn't mind dropping you off for graduation ceremony rehearsal.

He leaned forward and kissed her on the cheek. "I knew I had to introduce myself when I walked into the bar."

She turned and the light hit him just right that he looked like Principle Grand. All her fears and doubts came back in that moment. She felt her heart race, and she knew she needed a moment to breathe. She leaned forward calmly. She kissed him on the cheek. "I need to go freshen up really quick."

"I hope you aren't scared of me," Richard said. He needed this moral boast for his ego. Wasn't that always the common occurrence with middle aged men? They needed to get with pretty girls just to make them feel better about themselves. That was probably why his wedding ring was left in his pocket. Hoped your wife was okay with this type of business dinner.

Delilah got up and walked into the bathroom. She leaned over the sink and tried to control her breathing. She splashed some water on her face, and she felt her emotions taking over. She felt like she didn't have control anymore. She opened her purse. She hated that she was still this girl. She pulled out a razor. She pressed the razor to her wrist, but she stopped.

She wanted nothing more than to drag that blade across her skin and release this pain. She stopped and thought about how she didn't want to be weak and useless anymore. She was done with people making her feel horrible about herself. It was why she joined The Revenged Queen family.

She took in one shakey breath and released it. She put the razor back in her purse, and she fixed her hair. She walked out of the room and took her seat across from Richard. "Sorry about that."

"Why don't we get out of here?" he asked. "I have a hotel right around the corner."

Delilah was in no mood to put out on the first meeting. She did the same thing with Principal Grand. You had to make them beg for it. She leaned over and grabbed a cocktail napkin. She pulled out a pen from her purse. She wrote down her number. She turned and handed it to him.

"I don't put out on the first date. It's tacky and crude. I wouldn't mind getting drinks or dinner with you." She got up from her seat. She leaned in close to his ear. "I always put out on the second, though," she whispered. She leaned back to see Richard's eyes beam with arousal. She giggled and walked away.

Delilah, we were proud of you for being this sex kitten to the older gentleman. We wondered how long this little ruse of yours would last. You thought you were done with your secrets getting out, but this was the perfect scandal to blow up the life you were trying so hard to build. Our only question was, who would find out about your new obsession?

****

"There must be a mistake. I've had near perfect grades all through high school. I've turned in homework on time, I've studied for every test, and I've been doing so many extra curriculars," Bethany said, looking at her guidance counselor. We didn't know ruining peoples' lives counted as an extracurricular activity.

Ms. Diop looked at her files. "You've been failing a lot of your history and calculus tests lately." She clicked on a couple of her other grades. "You've been doing subpar in your other classes too. Yes, you've been pulled in a bunch of different directions, but you will not be valedictorian of Johnson Prep class of 2019."

Bethany smiled. "Once again, there must be a mistake."

Ms. Diop turned the computer around for her to see. "I don't make mistakes. I just show you the facts. Have you been distracted lately?" she asked.

Bethany touched her stomach. "No, I haven't." She stood up. "Is there any chance I can still be valedictorian?"

"Unless you get your teachers to raise these grades, and you somehow get the other student who is number one right now to fail, I don't see you being valedictorian." Ms. Diop was okay with Bethany not being valedictorian. She thought she was a complete bitch, and she was constantly needy.

"I'll make sure I get my grades up." She walked out of the guidance office trying to keep it together.

Bethany, were you as dumb as Delilah? Should you be getting extra help with your classes? We heard the best way to get your grades up was fucking the principal. Too bad you exposed that secret and couldn't use that method.

She bumped into Danielle outside of the office. Danielle was on her way to her next video meeting with an older gentleman. Danielle looked to see it was Bethany. She saw that she was clearly upset. "You okay?" she asked.

Bethany saw that it was Danielle. "What's it to you? Shouldn't you be busy cleaning your trailer park?"

Danielle laughed and crossed her arms. "It's so funny that's the only thing you can say now. Look at the bitch that thought she was above it all."

"I am, because I'm The Marked Queen."

"That doesn't make you above it. It makes you the center. You think you're better than everyone around here, but we all know it's bullshit." Danielle paused for a moment.

"You also thought you were better than everyone. I'm humble."

"Are you? You think no one's going to come for you after what you did at prom? That's a stupid ideology."

Bethany thought of The Revenged Queen. She didn't know if Danielle had it in her to attack her. "Are you saying you're coming for me? I didn't know Cinderella could be so mean." Bethany paused. "Well you have the poor look down, but I doubt you have the heart of gold."

"It's going to be so great to see you fall. You think your secrets are safe. You believe you're untouchable. We all thought that for so long, then you came around. We all saw how well that worked for all of us." Danielle knew Bethany needed to be knocked down, and she was going to cheers the bitch that does it. Danielle, we wouldn't break out the glassware just yet. We heard you were going to be a part of that blast too.

"Are you declaring war on me?"

Danielle shrugged. "I don't need to. I've hung up the cap for being part of the bitch war." Danielle looked around. "There are enough girls in here willing to take you down."

"I'll find more dirt on them."

"But you don't get it. There all looking for dirt on you. You think your house is made of bricks, but we all know it's made of paper."

"How so?"

"Because it's Johnson Prep." Danielle looked at her watch. "I better get going. Have fun with your day, Bethany. Can't wait to see you burn, bitch." Danielle waved and walked away from her.

Bethany thought back to the dream she had during her abortion. She clung to her stomach, and she felt like it was all falling apart. She walked into the bathroom and locked the door. She fell to the ground and began to breakdown. She had hit her breaking point. She had gotten an abortion to keep her reputation intact, she was slowly losing Tucker, and she was no longer top of her class.

"Why did I have to be The Marked Queen?" she asked out loud. She knew no one was in here. She remembered what her mother said about making memories in this school, and she knew that she would only have prom as a highlight.

Aw Bethany, we wanted to relate to you, but we weren't horrible bitches. We applauded you for your performance at prom, but did you really believe people would be friends with you after? You had treated your boyfriend and Susan as punching bags. You were worse than any of the bullies in this school. You thought people loved the bullies, but they were the biggest losers of them all.

"I'll be on top," she said to herself. She got up from the floor. She walked over to the sink and pulled herself together. She was just another mean girl that was hiding behind a mask. She wanted to believe she was loved by the masses, but would soon realize you were even worse off than being a wallflower. Hoped you loved your rise to the "top," because once you get there, you would have no one cheering for you. Well, except for the people dying to see you fall to your death.

Chapter 24

"Are you seriously on Grindr at a baseball game?" Danielle asked. Calvin had asked her to come to this stupid game to support his team. She had plans to meet with one of her older clients tonight. Christian thought it was time she got paid the big bucks, and that was in escorting. Who would have thought our darling Danielle was good at something other than sewing and being a bitch?

Calvin looked at the picture of the guy he was here to see play. He was Johnson Prep's opponent in the semi-finals. "I'm actually here for the outfielder," Calvin said. He showed Danielle the photo.

Danielle looked at the photo and the guy currently working out. "You don't wait long, do you?"

Calvin shrugged. "I decided to get this hook up app a try. People do it all the time." Calvin, you were only on it because you decided to lock your heart out to the others. You were being a stereotypical gay, and we weren't complaining. Hoped you enjoy spreading your legs pretending it was love.

"I'm worried about you. Are you sure you should be doing this?"

Calvin looked Danielle up and down. "You look fancy for a baseball game."

"Touché."

"I'm having fun. I spent almost all year trying to get Aman to come out for me. I have two weeks left in this school. I might as well have fun in the process."

Danielle seemed skeptical. She pulled out her lipstick. "There's nothing wrong with a little fun, but I don't need you completely falling apart. We don't need another basket case. Don't you remember Andrew?"

"I think alcohol was involved, and besides there's nothing wrong with a steamy locker room scene." Calvin scrolled up to show Danielle his plan once the game was over.

She nodded in approval. "This Calvin seems so much more fun."

He blushed and looked coy. "I'm trying very hard."

They watched the game. Calvin tried to keep his arousal down when he saw the guy go up to bat. He tried to imagine him outside of his baseball uniform, and he couldn't wait to see him under hot water. Calvin didn't care who won the game; he was ready to give the guy any award he deserved.

The game had ended, and people started leaving. "I'll leave you to your session," Danielle got up.

"You going to be okay getting home?" Calvin asked.

Danielle turned to see her private car showing up. "I think I'll be fine." She leaned down and kissed Calvin on the cheek. "Have fun." She walked away from the bleachers.

Calvin waited an hour or so at the bleachers. He got a notification from Noah, the outfielder, to come to the locker room. Everyone had left, and he had the place to himself. Calvin left the bleachers and slipped in through the door toward the locker room.

He walked into the locker room where everyone had obviously left. "Hello?" he asked out loud. He was nervous someone was going to attack him.

Noah came out of the showers. His olive skin shinned from the light coming into the locker room. His blonde hair was slicked back by the water. Calvin took in a dry gulp from looking at Noah's thick body in person. "I've been dying to get you in here."

Calvin walked over and pulled Noah into a kiss. It was filled with lust. Noah and Calvin began to get aroused. Noah looked at Calvin. "You going to take those clothes off or what?"

Calvin chuckled. He quickly took off his clothes as they began to make out. They took their quick romance to the shower. They explored their bodies with tongues, lips, and teeth. Calvin, you were becoming an adventurous slut. We were beginning to notice that condoms weren't on your list of supplies. We hoped it didn't bite you in the ass.

Calvin, you should have learned to be quiet or the coach wouldn't be in the locker room wondering where all that sound was coming from. "Noah, are you alone in here?"

Calvin quickly tried to hide away. Noah came out of the corner of the shower with a hard on. "I didn't know I couldn't masturbate in the shower."

The coach turned the other way. "I don't need to know about your private time in here. Finish up. I'm just glad I didn't see you with a girl," he said. He walked out of the locker room.

Noah walked back into the shower. "Sorry about that."

"So, you're not out?" Calvin asked. He just assumed from the coach's comments.

Noah laughed. "I'm not stupid. I'm trying to get to the major leagues. Of course, I'm staying in the closet. I don't want to end up like you."

Nothing said boner-killer like bringing up your slam piece's demise. "What's that supposed to mean?" Calvin asked.

"You were one of the top catchers in the city. You came out, and you got kicked off your team during playoffs."

"I only got kicked off because someone called me a faggot."

"You're proving my point. It's why I'll stay in the closet." Noah leaned forward and tried to kiss Calvin.

Calvin placed a hand on Noah's naked chest. Aw, you shouldn't have felt bad for what he said, Calvin. We wanted you to continue letting him get his victory boner out on you. We wanted sex, not feelings. "I think we're done here."

"Are you seriously upset about me staying in the closet?"

"No, I'm pissed off that you're saying my life is falling apart after I came out."

Noah tried not to sound like a dick. "Hasn't it, though?"

Calvin didn't answer the question because he knew the fucking truth. You were trying to figure out your label, but we had already figured it out for you. Weren't you supposed to be the successful and popular one? Turns out, you were as fucked up as the rest of us.

"Fuck this." Calvin walked out of the shower. He quickly put his clothes on and got out of the locker room. He leaned against the wall once he left. Did you feel used, abused, and taken advantage of? You were trying to run away from the truth, but it was just delivered in the form of a hot, closeted baseball player. We would say it was you, but he had the smarts to keep his secrets behind closed doors. He was right, though. Your life was falling apart, and we were here cheering for it with wine and popcorn. Calvin, we didn't want you to worry too much, you still had time for your rock bottom.

****

Danielle looked out the window. She was listening to Christian tell her about the older gentleman she was planning to have dinner with tonight. He was paying her over a grand for an evening with her. She looked at Christian and smiled. "I never would have suspected you would be my pimp, when I met you a couple months back at the gala."

Christian smiled. He leaned over and took a line of coke. "I knew there was something about you that made me think we would meet again."

"Desperation?"

He shook his head. "No, survival. I'll never judge anyone for what they're doing on this website. I've been there too. It's surprising how many rich kids are on this site to get back at their parents."

She took a sip of her drink as they drove toward the restaurant. "Until their parents pay enough money to get their child off the sites."

Christian laughed. "Where do you think my yearly bonus comes from?"

"Does your dad know this is the business you're involved in?"

"My dad doesn't care how I build my empire, as long as I make it." Christian knew his father wouldn't approve of the actual product, but he couldn't deny the money figures. He was doing what his father wanted, and he was enjoying the dirty, dark side of the world. He was getting the best of both.

"It must be nice to have a parent so hands off."

"I'm assuming your mother doesn't know where you're getting the cash," Christian said.

"She thinks that I'm working at a nice restaurant in The Upper East Side. She thinks that now everyone knows I'm poor, that I can work wherever I want."

"If that was the case, you would have never contacted me."

Danielle looked at him. "You know damn well that I'm not going to serve those pathetic wannabes at Johnson Prep."

Danielle would rather kill herself than be caught dead serving her classmates. We guessed that getting the old perverted men off was way better.

"How's the boyfriend with everything?"

Danielle opened her mouth and turned to look outside again. "He's not an issue."

Christian was intrigued. He always thought she was attractive, and he wouldn't mind seeing her naked. He knew she had a boyfriend, and he didn't want to impose. He had some morals. Yes, you were whoring yourself to the world, but being a cheater was where you drew the line. We were proud of you. "So, no more?"

She grabbed her drink and finished it and slammed the glass down. "I don't need anyone judging me for my actions. I know how I'm surviving in this world. I'm trying to make sure I have a home. I get that my mother has an issue with her pride, but I don't. People can all fuck themselves if they think I'm going to let them dictate my life."

Christian came to sit next to her. He handed her a rolled up hundred. "Why not play around fully then?"

"Shouldn't I be sober for this?" she asked.

He looked at her confused. "Why would you want to? It's some weird fifty-year-old that has a pact with his best friend to hang with younger girls. His friends are doing it the more dignified way." Christian rolled his eyes.

She took the bill out of his hand. "You have a problem with that?"

"I don't believe in morals or justification. No one should have dignity. It's so much more refreshing to give up on being a better human being."

Danielle knew he had a good point, and she felt a weight lift from her. She leaned down and snorted a line of coke. That was our popular girl. You once said that coke was for the bottom dwellers. It seemed you finally accepted your role in society, whore.

Christian and Danielle looked at each other for a moment. There was alcohol and cocaine coursing through their veins. They both didn't have anything to lose, and they were having a good time. Danielle thought about this moment rather than a date with a guy that paid for her. She pulled on his shirt and their lips crushed together.

Christian took control of the situation, once he realized what was going on. Their lips moved together in a sloppy fashion. You would think these two hotties would know how to make out a little less sloppily. Christian ran his hands up Danielle's thighs. She felt aroused. Dan, you should have been taking notes here, maybe that was why she dumped your judgmental ass.

The car came to a stop. Christian broke up the kiss. "Sorry to stop this as it was getting good. We are here, and I'm not going to piss off a client."

Danielle fixed her hair and looked at her make up in her compact mirror. "That was better to think about than him." She turned to open the door.

Christian grabbed her hand. "I'll wait for you."

Danielle turned to look at him. "Why? You always told me that the chase was way more fun." She got out of the limo. "I'll see you around." She winked as she closed the door.

Danielle took in a deep breath. She touched her lips and smiled. She knew nothing would ever happen with him. He was a walking red flag. She knew he was sexy, and he knew how to control a situation, but she would never be special to him. Fuck romance, Danielle. You have had your fairytale, and it didn't work out. You better get back in the limo, take off your dress, and let that sexy ass make you scream in more ways than one. We wished you weren't so focused on building a life for yourself. We prayed you didn't go into that building for this arranged date. If you turned and went back into the limo with Christian, then your scandal would have been kept safe.

Chapter 25

"Alright, class I decided that I wanted to do a fun project this week," Ms. Cornwall said to her class. "There are half seniors and half juniors in this class. Since it's AP study hall, and all the AP tests are done for the year, I thought we do a little project before we send the seniors off next week. I'm going to pair each of the juniors with a senior. The juniors, I want you to ask for advice from the seniors about finishing senior year, and the seniors, I want you to ask how your class has influenced the junior class." Ms. Cornwall, we could answer that question for you. Didn't you remember prom from a couple weeks back?

Jordan looked bored of this assignment already. She just wanted to spend the next couple of weeks taking down Bethany. She thought it was rather odd that graduation was next week. She smiled because after next week, she would be the new queen in town.

Ms. Cornwall said everyone's pairings. Jordan hadn't ever heard of an Alassane before. Alassane came sitting next to Jordan. He had caramel skin, a nice smile, was in shape, with brown eyes, and his famous accessory was a brace on his left leg. "Sup, Jordan," Alassane said sitting next to her.

Jordan looked at him. She thought he was cute and clearly looked like her type, but she wasn't sure if she had slept with him before. "Do I know you?"

"I've been to a couple of your parties."

It didn't ring a bell. "And by parties...." She let him finish the sentence.

He chuckled. "Don't worry, I wasn't part of your sex parties. I'm not that type of athlete."

Jordan was confused. If he wasn't on the lacrosse or football team, what sport did he play? "What kind of athlete are you?"

"Gymnastics."

It clicked in her head why she didn't know him. No one gave a shit about the gymnasts in this school, unless you were a horny male. "Ah, you're gay."

"Actually straight. I had a huge crush on your friend, Delilah White for a while."

"Really? Why didn't you ever make a move on her?"

"What's with the twenty questions?" Alassane leaned forward and raised an eyebrow.

Jordan hated how cute he looked in the moment. She just assumed he was only interested in her because she was easy. "I'm just trying to get to know you. Isn't that part of the assignment?"

"I don't think it's part of it, but I'll answer the question. I'm best friends with Flynn."

"Hope you mean ex, after the shit he pulled with her."

"Hey, I think what he did was a douche move, but he didn't deserve to be humiliated in front of the whole school."

"Blame The Marked Queen."

"Don't worry, she's not a fan in my book. I think she's a huge bitch. I had a couple classes with her. She didn't think I was smart enough to do any partner projects with her." He crossed his arms.

She thought it was cute how he got when he was angry. "You done being dramatic over there?"

"And another thing. Just because I'm a gymnast doesn't mean I'm stupid, and I have no future in fashion design," Alassane added. He remembered an argument Bethany and him got into about a project they did in their English class. They were supposed to write an essay on the other person, and Alassane said he wanted to be a fashion designer. Bethany responded that was a stupid career.

"So, you're a gymnast, and you want to become a fashion designer. I'm pretty sure you're gay."

Alassane rolled his eyes. "Fuck off."

Jordan laughed, and it was the first time she felt like she could breathe. This guy wasn't looking at her like a giant whore bimbo, who has nothing going for her other than her loose vagina. We all knew that was true, but it was refreshing for someone to see her in a different light.

"You have a beautiful laugh," he said. He knew what her reputation was, and he wasn't trying to get caught up in that mess. He didn't find any romantic chemistry with her, but he felt some platonic feelings.

She blushed and looked away from him. "I think that's the first time someone has ever given me a compliment before."

"Well, I'm glad to give you one," he said.

There was a cute moment that made us barf. They went on to work on their projects together, and Jordan felt relaxed in this situation. She felt like she didn't have to put on a mask, and she was able to push all her problems to the side. It was good to see The Revenged Queen finding friendship right before her day as judge. Hoped he could stand you once he realized you were just like The Marked Queen.

****

Danielle walked down the tables in the cafeteria to her table with Calvin. She walked past all the clichés in the school. You could say that you saw the hierarchy of the school. Danielle and

Calvin were tossed to the side once their scandals came out. Aman, Jordan, Emily, and Delilah all sat at the top table. It had to suck for Bethany, because she still sat at the wallflower table. Wasn't that a bitch?

Danielle was walking to her table, when Susan was getting up from a table with her new group of friends. They were the nerds of the school known for newspaper, broadcasting, and yearbook. They took care of showing off the memories, but they weren't in any of them. Bethany was their queen, until she tossed them to the side for a chance at the royal court.

Susan smiled at Danielle. Danielle could tell that she had a lot of confidence. She was pleased to see she had made some new friends. "I see things have worked out for you after dumping Bethany and Tucker."

Susan turned to them and smiled. "It's nice to have friends who aren't trying to blackmail me into doing their bidding." Susan thought of Jasmine and Bethany.

"It's good to actually have a genuine friendship with people," Danielle said.

"Friendship. Isn't that ironic coming from your mouth?" Delilah asked, walking up next to Danielle.

Danielle turned to Delilah. She rolled her eyes. She had come to accept that she would never be friends with Delilah again, but it didn't mean she wasn't annoyed with Delilah bringing up prom. "Don't you have other people to harass?" Danielle asked. She pointed to Bethany. "You could go call her a bitch if you wanted."

Delilah crossed her arms. "Why would I go after Bethany? If you really think about it, you caused The Marked Queen."

"What?" Susan asked. She looked confused.

"Yes, Susan. You, Bethany, Tucker, and our bitch right here, Danielle all caused The Marked Queen."

"How did I create The Marked Queen?" Danielle asked. She was curious about Delilah's theories.

"You were the one that bullied Bethany so much. You made fun of her, created the pranks, and you beat her self-esteem down. She had to retaliate, and she created the persona."

Danielle laughed and rolled her eyes. "You must love playing the victim. I'm not a villain, you whiny bitch. You were having as much fun as I was making fun of Bethany. You aren't this sweet angel." Danielle paused. "You did sleep with the principal after all."

Delilah felt enraged. She got into Danielle's face. "I trusted you, and you backstabbed me."

"We get it. I was a bitch to you. We've all done horrible things. Why don't you stop being the hurt sidekick and get over it?" Danielle looked Delilah straight in the eyes.

"You act like you're better than all of us."

"I never thought I was better than any of you. I'm fucking honest. Yes, I was popular, and I made everyone believe I was rich. I know my faults, and I know what I've done. My secrets are out in the open."

Danielle, we were pretty sure no one knew you were a high-class escort.

"I doubt it." Delilah leaned into Danielle's ear. "I can't wait to bring you down," she whispered.

"That's fine, Delilah. It just proves how pathetic your life is that you continue to be obsessed with mine. Once again, you were always meant to be the sidekick and nothing more." Danielle stood her ground.

"Fuck off." Delilah felt her emotions building up. "I'll go sit at the high table now." She turned and walked away.

"Which is funny, since no one gives two shits about you since we all found out you were the principal's cum dumpster," Danielle screamed out.

Delilah stopped for a moment. She looked around and saw that people were looking at her. She could breakdown right then, but she wouldn't. She wouldn't give Delilah that satisfaction. She held her head high and walked away. She knew Danielle wouldn't be so smug when The Revenged Queen was done with her.

"Why be so mean to her?" Susan asked.

"It's Johnson Prep. We don't do forgiveness that easily," Danielle said. She knew it would be a long road until she and Delilah would be friends again. She missed her best friend, and she still regretted what she did.

"Don't you think it's better to be the bigger person?" she asked.

Danielle turned to Susan. "You would need to change the system first. It's what has always been the art of the game." She paused. "I'm happy you found friends. Let's hope they aren't as cruel as us." She gave Susan a weak smile before sitting with Calvin.

Susan was left standing there wondering how this school could be so vicious to their classmates. Susan, you couldn't have been that stupid. You saw the true evil of Jasmine and Bethany. You also knew they were keeping up masks to protect their vulnerable sides. We hoped you learned that in a bitch war, you keep the tears behind the closed doors and save the villainous laughs for the masses.

Chapter 26

Calvin was in his room on Grindr looking for someone else to distract him. Noah had tried to message him again, but he ignored him. He didn't want to relive the fact that Noah had told him he made a mistake coming out. Calvin continued to scroll, and he found Terrell's profile. He quickly rushed past that one too. Didn't you hate the gay community? You tried to escape the mistakes of your past, but you were all thirsty whores.

Aubrey came walking into Calvin's room. She took a seat on the bed and looked at her son. "Having fun?" she asked.

Calvin looked at his mom. "I don't know what you're talking about."

She smiled weakly. "Sleeping around and drinking. This isn't the son I raised."

He slid up. "I've been with Danielle a lot lately."

The Grindr notification went off. It was a message from a headless torso. Aubrey wasn't stupid. She knew what that sound was. She had studied the gay culture when Calvin came out. "So, you aren't on a hook up app right now?"

"I can't have a healthy sex life?" he asked. "I thought you guys would be supportive of my lifestyle."

"You call this a lifestyle?" she asked. She reached over and grabbed his phone.

Calvin freaked out, because there were messages in there that he didn't want his mom to find out about. "Mom, you can't."

She glared at him. "I pay for your cell phone bill. You might legally be an adult, but I'll be going through your shit until you go off to college." She started reading some of the messages guys sent her son. Aubrey, you should take them as compliments. You created a son that all the boys wanted to play with. You go, girl.

She looked at him. She nodded and handed him the phone. "Are you being protective?"

"What?" he asked.

"Are you using condoms?" she asked.

Calvin thought about it. Him and Aman always used condoms. Terrell and him, he wasn't so sure. He knew he and Omar didn't. When he was with Noah, he didn't really get aroused for him to enjoy it, but he didn't remember if they used a condom or not. Calvin, you were creating quite a list, and we wished it was longer. "Sometimes yes and sometimes no."

She shook her head and stood up. "I wish you had your act together. You're sleeping around, you got kicked off the baseball team, and you seem like you've completely lost yourself."

He stood up. "I don't know what you want from me. I'm trying to figure out this world now that I am out."

"By having your mouth on every cock you see?" she asked.

He was quiet for a moment. "I just want to know that it's okay to be in this community." He didn't want to admit that he was trying to find love when Aman tossed his ass to the side. Calvin, you ruined that by coming out. We applauded you for your bravery, but you knew you weren't good enough for him to leave his culture.

Aubrey knew he was still hurting from his breakup from Aman. She stepped forward. "You don't need to sleep around because you have a broken heart."

He shook his head. "It has nothing to do with Aman."

"You two broke up only a couple of weeks ago."

"But we were having problems way before then. We were never going to work out." Calvin felt himself starting to fall apart. "He decided that I wasn't worth enough to him. Do you know how much I wish I could go back into that cage with him? I had my boyfriend, and I had a life. People didn't label me for my sexuality."

"You know deep down that you were truly unhappy. You were living a half-life. If you were complete, you wouldn't have come out. It's hard. I'll never know what it's like to be you, Calvin. What I do know is that you're more relaxed. You're going through some troubles, but you aren't crying yourself to sleep anymore."

"Mom," Calvin said. She had a point, Calvin. There were so many nights you cried wondering if you were ever going to be stronger than this. You were hurt that you loved someone that couldn't love you back. You had a weight on yourself, and you felt like it would never come off.

"Calvin, you've always been my sweet boy. You've been strong, independent, and I've been inspired by you. You have been keeping your true self away from the world. You can now be unapologetically you."

"I miss him. I can't seem to get my footing back."

"Because you thought the only person that could love you was him. You don't need to hide anymore."

"Then why does every guy I've been with only want my body? They get to know me. They don't care if I'm broken, scared, nervous, and lonely. They just want a quick fuck." Calvin wanted nothing more than for Terrell to be somewhat of a beacon for him, but he had a rude awakening from that experience.

"I will never tell you that you're going to escape horrible people. You need to keep your heart open. You need to believe that it's going to be okay. I truly believe you'll find someone that will give you all you need." She touched his face. "I want you to keep fighting, and I want you to stop being a coward."

"How so?"

"Sleeping around with useless boys. You need to build a career for yourself. You're about to enter the real world in a couple of weeks. You're graduating, and my job is done. I've taught you all that I can. Please, I need you to realize the mistakes you're making. It could ruin your life."

He chuckled. "I ruined my life when I told The Marked Queen about Aman and I." He grabbed his jacket and phone. "I'm just trying to numb the pain now." He walked out of the room. He got on Grindr, and a guy wanted him to come to the club.

Calvin left knowing that he was disappointing everyone around him. Calvin, when would you learn that you had to love yourself before you could be truly happy? We knew it was cliché, but it was the Hallmark bullshit we were trying to achieve here. We wanted you to find love with the fact that all you would be was a thirst trap with no intelligence or morals. You were just like Danielle, except she was paid for her time.

****

Jordan swayed to the music as she danced on the dance floor. She had guys coming up to her, and she ignored them. She just wanted to enjoy the noise. She hated coming home from school to find once again an empty house. Val had gone away on a quick trip with some friends. She tried to get some friends to come over, but they were too busy. She thought of asking Alassane to come over, but she knew that would make her too clingy. She didn't even know if she had feelings for him.

She turned to see the bartender smiling at her. She thought he was cute, and she hadn't taken home a bartender yet. She walked over to the bar and ordered herself some shots. She leaned over the bar showing off her tits. Jordan, we thought you had more class than that. Who were we kidding, you show those tits, girl. We knew you would fuck him right there on the bar. You loved a good audience.

She took a shot and turned to see Calvin flirting with some guy. He had blonde hair and was skinny. She couldn't see his face. They kissed, and the guy walked away. Calvin had a smile on his face, until he made eye contact with Jordan. His heart dropped to his stomach.

He tried to run away, but she was walking right toward him. "I never thought Mr. All American would be caught at a night club like this," Jordan said.

He finished his drink. "I guess you really don't know me." He crossed his arms. "Don't you have parties to reject people from?"

She rolled her eyes. She signaled to the bartender for couple more shots. "That was all Delilah's doing. She has a massive grudge against your best friend."

The bartender placed two tequila shots down. They both took one. "Danielle didn't do Delilah any favors."

"So, you think Danielle was in the wrong?"

"I think what she did was wrong, but we were all trying to keep our secrets from getting out."

"Except you."

He laughed. "We all saw how well that worked for me." He signaled for two more shots. He just wanted to forget his conversation with his mother. He saw the sheer disappointment on her face, and he didn't want to relive that again.

"Someone is on a mission to get drunk tonight."

"I'd rather not go back to my place."

"How so?" she asked.

"I remembered after the Aman situation blew up in my face, to keep everything close to my chest.' He didn't know if he could trust Jordan. She was a dark horse, and he didn't need his problems to get out.

"Why don't we make a deal? These are neutral waters. We don't talk about Johnson Prep. We dance and flirt with boys."

Calvin was interested. He didn't really have a friend to go out with. He wanted to escape everything, and he needed a partner in crime. "I do need someone to help me get a cutie. It makes me look desperate coming here all the time."

Jordan laughed. "Hey, we are both sluts."

"At least I didn't gang bang the football team."

She picked up her shot glass. "Aw, but the faggot wanted to, didn't he?"

He picked up his shot glass. "I hate that you think I'm a stereotypical gay."

"But you assume that I'm a stereotypical whore."

"Touché." They cheered to their new arrangement.

They ended up on the dance floor trying to escape their problems. Calvin slowly forgot about the conversation that he and his mother had. He wanted to be lost in this world, and he prayed that people would love him on the other side. He just didn't have to worry about it right now.

Jordan wasn't the girl stuck in a quiet home. She found someone to escape with. She had never expected it to be with Calvin, but this was Johnson Prep. Everyone had new alliances forming every single day.

They broke to get some air after thirty straight minutes of dancing. The blonde boy that Calvin was talking to came over to see if he wanted to get out of there. "Let me talk to my friend real quick." He walked over to Jordan. "You going to be okay if I leave?" Calvin asked.

Jordan looked over at the guy waiting for Calvin. "Yes, you better get out of here with him." Jordan could tell that the bartender was still eyeing her down.

Calvin looked over to see the bartender was eye fucking her. "You seem to have your plans for the evening."

Jordan giggled. "What can I say?"

"I'd like to do this again. It's our own dirty secret."

"That must be nice."

He leaned forward and kissed her on the cheek. "I hope you were able to escape your problems for the night with me," she said.

She grabbed his hand. She squeezed it because he had no clue how much she needed tonight. It was innocent fun, but it was something she could hold on to. She didn't get consumed by the voices and betrayal from herself. "You have no idea."

Calvin felt the blonde boys hand on his ass. "Yes, you did. I better get going before he gets impatient." He turned and grabbed the guy's hand. They left into the chill night knowing they were going to have a long evening.

Our sluts have officially become best friends. We hoped they could teach other about the lovely infections they were both going to endured. We prayed you two didn't get your morals anytime soon. We were wondering how this friendship would last, especially when your two best friends hated each other. Boys and girls, we were about to see a grand showdown, who would these two whores chose to defend?

Chapter 27

Wasn't it a shame, Lily? We knew you wanted your daughter to succeed, but we didn't think you meant in this way. How did it feel seeing your daughter show all her best qualities online? We understood that you didn't believe Dan in the beginning, but weren't you thrilled you believed him now?

Lily turned to see Danielle walk in the door. "How could you?" she asked.

Danielle looked at her confused. She thought she had work, and she was supposed to have another internet session. "Mom, what are you doing home?"

Lily turned the laptop toward her daughter. "I had work, but it seemed that something came up."

Danielle walked over to the computer to see what her mom was talking about. She closed the laptop when she came on the screen in just black lingerie. "Mom, I can explain."

Lily crossed her arms. "I'm glad to see the lingerie I bought you for your birthday is going to good use. Yes, why don't you explain to me what in the fuck is going on here?"

"I was trying to get us out of debt, trying to keep a roof over our heads."

"So, you didn't get that job on The Upper East Side?"

"I'd rather kill myself than serve my classmates." Danielle, what would you do once they found out about this? We bet you wished you had just stuck to serving.

"Once again, you're caring what your peers are saying about you. I thought we were over this bullshit when you were exposed at prom. I thought you had matured."

"I don't give a damn that we are poor," Danielle said, "but I do care if we have a place to live."

"That's not what it looks like, with you stripping on the fucking screen for cash like a whore."

"And you weren't complaining when I gave you that cash." Danielle laughed. "I'm cleaning up your fucking mistakes."

Lily walked over to her daughter. "I thought we were past all of this."

"You make me have morals and take the high road. It's nice when you have a place to stay. It's called survival. I'm not ashamed that I'm showing the world my body. We paid our rent, and I'm saving for college. That's more than I can say about you."

"I will not be spoken to like this in my house."

"Really? It seems I'm the one fronting the fucking bill. Isn't that a bitch? Shouldn't you be taking care of me? I guess you never really stopped being the spoiled housewife"

Lily slapped her daughter across the face. "I have been trying for years to prove to you and this world that I made the right decision."

Danielle ignored the pain. She gave her mother a wicked grin. "And you're doing a terrible job of it. You have let your pride get in the way too many times."

"No, but I do have standards."

"Call them what you want, but we all know it's bullshit. I took our situation into my own hands, and I was getting what we needed done, done." She paused because she had a question for her mother. "How did you find out about this?" she asked.

"Dan told me."

Danielle should have figured out it was Dan. Danielle, we told you about the stable boy. Once you threw him to the curb, he had no loyalty to you. He was turning out to be an annoying wasp ruining you at every turn. You shouldn't have been with him in the first place. We understood you were trying to be a good person, but how did that work out?

"He really can't get a life of his own, can he?"

"He's worried about you."

"No, you both are trying to turn me into the perfect daughter and girlfriend. Don't you get it? That's not realistic and that's not what I fucking want."

"You can be if you stop with these antics," Lily said. She wanted nothing more than for her daughter to stop going down this dark path. Lily, you were being so stupid. Danielle finally got her claws back, and we missed this bitch.

"No, you both want to control me. I get that you think this is where it's better to be, but it's all bullshit. I'm doing what I need to do now to have a better future later."

"This will haunt you. Why can't you see that?" Lily asked.

Danielle shrugged. She didn't see the point of being ashamed of her accomplishments. Lily, she did have a point there. She was quickly becoming a rising star on the fetish website. You should be proud of your daughter. "I'm done listening to you and the reject next door. I'm still making my clothes. I'm still being humble, but I accepted reality. If you want to survive in this world, you have to play in the mud."

"What about Parsons? I bet they won't accept a prostitute into the school?"

"I doubt they would care, but if they do? Fuck them then. I'll do it my way." She grabbed her purse. She would record at Christian's house. He always talked about doing a video together. "I'll have the finances to make it. Hope your dignity keeps you warm once you get evicted from this dump." She walked toward the door.

"I've never seen you lose your way like this. It kills me to see you doing this."

Danielle turned to her mother. "What? I finally don't give a damn what people think of me. I thought you would be proud of me for that." She opened the door. "Don't you wish you had the daughter that was just worried about getting her social reputation back? You and Dan caused this, so you both can cry to each other."

Danielle walked out of that house not worrying about her mother's words. She wasn't going to let anyone control her again. Danielle had finally enjoyed freedom, and it was quite a divine taste. You believed that you didn't care what people thought of you, but we would ask you the same question once the graduation ceremony happened. Hoped you enjoyed having new fans and enemies after it was all said and done.

****

Tucker was in the photo lab trying to wrap his mind around the bomb that Bethany dropped on him. He was trying to find reasoning in why she would give up their child without even talking to him about it first. He sighed heavily, because he just wanted his girlfriend back. He thought once The Marked Queen was exposed, they would get back to who they were.

He heard a knock on the door. He wasn't developing film yet. He opened the door to see who it was. Emily walked in. "I haven't heard from you in a couple of days."

"Yeah, I had a busy weekend. I was trying to wrap my head around some things," he said.

Tucker, we understand that you wanted to be a dad, but you had other worries right now. Elizabeth reappearing being the biggest of those issues.

She looked at him. "What's going on?" she asked.

He wanted to tell her, but it wasn't his secret to tell. "I can't right now."

She leaned against the table. She could tell that something was eating him up inside. "You do know that you can trust me, right?"

He looked at her and laughed. "I don't think I can trust anyone in this school. We've all created personas of backstabbing villains." He placed the film in the developing water.

"There are good people in this school." She reached over and touched his hand. "I feel like the past couple of weeks we've gotten to know and trust each other."

He turned to look at her. He would never deny his attraction for Emily. He thought she was misinterpreted because of this school. He had the same blood on his hands too.

He thought of Bethany in that moment. "Yes." He pulled his hand away. Tucker, why did you have to be a good person? We knew that you were trying to make up for the sins of that night, but Elizabeth saw you as an evil person. Why not prove her right?

She crossed her arms. She was disappointed he was brushing off her advances. How far did you have to go to want to sleep with a mouth breather? Emily, were starting to worry about you. "What's going on?"

He turned to look at Emily. "I feel like my relationship with Bethany has all been a lie."

"Power does go to people's head."

"I never thought she would turn out like Danielle," Tucker said. We didn't agree with that statement. Danielle was a heartless overachiever that we loved. Bethany was a bitch that we would rather ignore.

"Danielle wouldn't have done what Bethany did."

He pulled the photo out of the water. It was a photo of Emily when she was reading in the library. Tucker, you were really giving off that stalker vibe. "She exposed Delilah's secrets. She exposed so many peoples lies."

"Because your girlfriend made them."

Tucker looked at Emily. "After Danielle bullied us. I guess no one remembers how horrible that bitch could be."

"Why are you bringing this up?" Emily asked.

Tucker thought of the abortion. "Because people would sacrifice everything to keep their reputation intact. You would think people didn't care. We are graduating next week."

"Some of us still have another year of this hell hole," Emily said. She wished she was graduating, and she had some freedom from this world. She was ready to run away, but she had no one to go with and nowhere to go.

Tucker gave her a weak smile. "It will be nice to leave these halls for the final time."

"Will you miss me?" Emily asked.

Tucker looked at Emily. "I wished I could say no." He knew his feelings for Emily were becoming inappropriate. He found comfort with her that he has never had before. He left the room because he couldn't be alone with her in there.

Emily looked at the photo. She touched it softly, and she felt her heart skip a beat. No one had done that for her. Andrew was too busy getting drunk and Mattew was too busy getting high. Tucker hasn't been busy killing anyone just yet.

She was furious. She left the room, and Tucker was still standing there. "You don't get to take beautiful photos of me and then brush me off."

Tucker looked at her. "We can't be together. I'm with Bethany."

"Do you even love her anymore?"

He opened his mouth and closed it. He hasn't been able to love her since she dropped the news about the abortion. "I don't think I can say I do."

She grabbed the front of his shirt. She was done playing these games with him. She wanted to be with him. She pulled him in, and he didn't stop her. Their lips met, filled with desire. Their lips moved together, and it seemed that the they really did deserve to be together.

It was truly sweet to see these two come together. The only issue was they were doing it out in the open. You might have wanted to make sure the door was closed. You didn't know who could be watching. It must be a bitch for you, Bethany. You were trying to make up with your boyfriend, and he was locking lips with the trashy girl from Johnson Prep. We assumed your pearls didn't do it for him anymore.

****

Tucker sat down next to Bethany and kissed her on the cheek. His mind was still swirling after his kiss with Emily. He knew that he needed to figure out his feelings for her before he told Bethany of it. "How are you?"

Bethany took a bite of her sandwich. She spent the last two periods thinking about how she would bring up Tucker kissing Emily. She thought she would make a big scene. She thought about keeping it close to her chest and ignoring it. She couldn't be dumped by her boyfriend. She was The Marked Queen, and she couldn't look like a loser.

She turned to see him with a smile on his face. She couldn't keep her anger in. "It's so nice to see you're smiling. It must be because you finally got to kiss Emily," she said, and took a sip of her water. Bethany, you knew how to be a cold bitch.

"What?" Tucker asked. He didn't think Bethany saw.

She smiled. "You didn't think anyone would catch you? Question, have you been licking the alcohol off her lips for some time now?"

"She kissed me."

"Isn't that what they always say. It was her, and I was the victim. If you ask me, that's all a bunch of bullshit. You wanted it as much as her. She wasn't the one in the relationship."

"It must suck being considered the one out of the loop," Tucker said.

"What's that supposed to mean?"

He leaned forward. "Abortion."

She leaned back. "You can't compare the two."

"Really? I think it's still the same level of betrayal."

She slapped him across the face. Bethany, you tried to keep it low-profile, but you now created an audience for yourself. "Fuck you. I did what I needed to do." She stood up.

"But you decided not to tell me about it."

"I did it for the both of us. I made sure that it wouldn't become an issue." She tried to keep the abortion as vague as possible. She knew people were watching them, and she couldn't let it out. Bethany, one of your audience members already knew about your secret. Carter was watching from the sidelines, and he was enjoying the show.

"But you didn't even tell me about it."

"Oh, like how you told me about your feelings for Emily?" People started to whisper to each other.

Tucker finally stood up. He turned to see Emily walking toward them. "I didn't know what I felt until we kissed."

"You told her?" Emily asked. She didn't think he would quickly run to his girlfriend about it.

"Don't worry, trash. I saw you two making out in the photo lab." She crossed her arms. "I'm not surprised. You've always gone after the weak."

Emily placed her lunch tray down. "I've never chosen the guys."

"No right-minded guy would want to date scum like you."

Emily felt enraged. She got in Bethany's face. "I'll show you how trashy I am."

"It shouldn't be shocking that you don't know the unwritten rule of this school. We don't use our fists, we use our smarts," Bethany laughed. "You never had any in the first place."

"At least, I have a heart."

"Really, because you sent a guy to rehab and a guy six-feet under. I don't know if that's very gracious of you."

Bethany, you were being one frigid bitch right now. Call out that trash, girl. She deserved it after she took your man. Where was Jerry Springer when you needed him?

"You think you're so much better than everyone since prom."

"I've always known I'm better than all of you," Bethany said. "I've never been caught up in drama, scandal, or backstabbing."

"But you wrote the book on it when you created The Marked Queen. You think people care for you. They despise you. You're nothing more than a wannabe social climber."

"And you're nothing more than a basket case with red flags written all over you."

Emily grabbed her tray. "Least guys are actually attracted to me."

"Doubtful."

"I don't know. You saw me and Tucker kiss. I felt the chemistry. I hope you did too." She brushed past Bethany to her seat. She knew Tucker could deal with that drama all on his own.

"This is the girl you decide to kiss," Bethany said.

"And this was the girl I dated. You have always believed you were better than everyone. You aren't perfect, Bethany. Why can't you just let the walls down? I've never felt like we truly connected."

"Is that why you kissed her?"

"Yes."

She slapped him across the face. "I want nothing to do with you anymore."

He nodded. "I think that's best. We haven't been us in so long. You have created this persona, and you have no remorse for what you've done." Tucker looked her in the eyes. "I want the girl I fell in love with to come back."

"She was weak," she said. Bethany hated the old her, and she would never be ashamed of the woman she was becoming. She had strength, courage, and she wouldn't let anyone let her go.

"But she had a heart." Tucker grabbed his things. "That was your best quality." He walked away leaving her humiliated in front of everyone.

Dumped in the town square. This just in, boys and girls. The Marked Queen had just lost her king in humiliating fashion. Was this newly crowned queen about to be kicked out of the kingdom for being a straight up wench? Careful Bethany, we wouldn't want you to have the same fate as the last reigning queen. We heard she was too busy being the kingdom's whore. At least she was worth a shilling or two, unlike your used-up ass. Have fun being the kingless queen no one wanted to fuck.

Chapter 28

He has had sex in different places, different positions, and with different sizes. The problem was, he wanted a connection with someone. Our piece of advice was to stop looking at photos of your ex and crying while jerking to them. It was beneath you, Calvin.

The nurse walked in to talk to Calvin. "What seems to be the problem?" she asked.

"I haven't been feeling well lately," Calvin said. He has been feeling tired, and lightheaded.

She nodded. She pulled out a thermometer to check his temperature. She also checked his ears, and his mouth. "Nothing seems to be out of the ordinary. Have you gone to the doctors?" she asked.

He shook his head. "No."

"Have you been sexually active?" she asked.

Calvin looked away from her. Calvin, you shouldn't be ashamed of how much you have been slutting it up. "Yes."

"Are you being protective?"

He looked at her. "Sometimes."

She nodded. "I think you need to go to the doctors to make sure you don't have any STI's."

At that moment Delilah walked into the nurse's office to ask for a tampon. "Sorry to interrupt."

The nurse looked at her. "I'm seeing another student. You can wait outside." She glared at her.

Delilah waved her hands in the air. "No problem." She closed the doors and squealed. She had stumbled upon dirt on Calvin. Who knew she would have had such luck? We were hoping you were wearing white today to give us a show, but this would be worth it instead.

The nurse turned to Calvin. "You need to be protective. You are all curious about your bodies, but that doesn't mean you're immune from anything." The nurse stood up. "Meet with a doctor and get tested."

Calvin moaned. "Great, that's something else I can worry about."

Calvin, you shouldn't have been surprised. You were throwing your ass around hoping someone would love you. We get that you found the gay world sexy, but they knew how to wrap it...most of the time. You were finally initiated into homosexuality. You were having your first STI scare. You shouldn't worry too much, you would have many more of these to come.

Calvin walked out of the nurse's office, and he bumped into Aman of all people. Aman looked up to see Calvin. "You okay?"

Calvin rolled his eyes. "Why is it you're the one that I always bump into?" Calvin, it was because karma was a bitch, and she wanted you to be reminded of how far you had fallen.

Aman reached out and tried to squeeze Calvin's hand. "Do you want to talk about it?" he asked.

Calvin saw Sana walking up to them. "Don't you have a girlfriend to please?"

Aman didn't get a chance to respond before Sana came up. "Shouldn't you be converting someone else?" Sana asked. It was quite adorable to see Sana try to lay claim to your man. Hasn't he told you that he still thinks of Calvin while you two were fucking?

Calvin raised his hands in the air. "I'm not trying to stir shit up. He bumped into me when I was leaving the nurse's office."

"Just like he was the one that kissed you in that photo?" Sana asked.

"Sana, you need to let that go." Aman didn't want Calvin to be beaten down more for that photo. He was over it, because his parents hadn't asked questions.

Calvin looked at him. "Your couple videos are doing great. I saw your recent one was trending. I'm happy for the both of you," Calvin said. He turned and walked away. He didn't want to deal with their drama or anything else that was going on.

Aman felt hurt watching Calvin walk away. He knew that there was nothing he could do. He caused all of this, and he wanted to believe that they would be friends at some point. Aman turned to Sana. "You don't need to be rude to him. He has done nothing wrong to you."

"Really? He humiliated your family and mine. Don't you get that you need to stay away from him?"

Aman knew he couldn't stay away from Calvin. He felt like a part of him was missing. He still felt a rush of excitement seeing Calvin, and he wanted to get back to that. "I can't with this right now."

Sana grabbed his arm. "We have a new video to record."

"Maybe I'm not in the film making mood."

"Too bad. This is what you're doing with your career." She leaned forward. "I might have given you a pass on that incident with Calvin, but it doesn't mean our families have fully forgotten."

Aman and Sana walked away, so they could figure out what they were going to do for their next video. It was a shame to see Aman still trapped in his rules with his family. You should also realize that it wasn't better coming out. Did this mean that our gay lovers should have stayed together? Who knew? But we had a feeling these two weren't done yet. Too bad for Aman, we didn't know if he would accept Calvin if he had something spreadable.

****

"I got the perfect scandal for Calvin," Delilah said, walking into an empty room where her and Jordan were supposed to meet.

Jordan had just talked to Carter about if Bethany had talked to him yet. She turned to see Delilah standing there. "And what would that be?" she asked.

"He might have an STI. He just met with nurse about how he hasn't been feeling well lately."

"Is it confirmed?" she asked.

"No, but I can use it against him to get dirt on Danielle." Delilah's main goal was to get Calvin to back stab her like Danielle did to Delilah.

Jordan nodded. "Perfect." She paused. "But I still need dirt on Bethany. Graduation is in a fucking week. We have nothing. This is becoming pointless."

"I think I can help with that," Emily said, walking into the room.

"Why are you here?" Delilah asked.

Jordan smiled. "She's the new member of the team."

"What? I thought it was going to be just us two." Aw Delilah, were you jealous that Jordan had another best friend? You shouldn't be sad. Everyone looked at you like second best.

Emily took a seat next to Delilah. "She ruined Andrew. She deserves to go down."

"You did that by giving him the bottle," Delilah said.

Emily stood up. "We could say the same about you getting on your knees."

Jordan rolled her eyes. She didn't need a pissing contest. She wanted this to go flawlessly, and she wanted The Revenged Queen to have her moment. "I don't need you two going after each other. Bethany built an army, and I want to do the same."

"Why not steal one of Bethany's members?" Emily asked.

"Susan?" Delilah asked.

"No. Tucker," Emily said, and Tucker walked in.

Jordan and Delilah both looked extremely uncomfortable with this. "He's her girlfriend," Jordan said.

"Not anymore." Tucker walked up to Emily and kissed her on the lips.

Jordan was stunned a little bit. She hadn't expected them to get romantic. Jordan, we were on the same page as you were. She used to go for hot guys with edge. Well, Tucker did have some edge to him. Hasn't he told you all about Elizabeth yet? He was a killer that got away with it. "This is unexpected."

"She isn't the girl that I fell in love with. I want to believe that she was doing this to stop."

"Why did you join?" Delilah asked.

Tucker turned to Emily and she stood up. "That's personal."

"We don't hide shit from each other," Delilah said.

Jordan rolled her eyes. She was getting annoyed with Delilah's bad girl attitude. "He killed a woman last year in a car accident. If you weren't too busy sucking the principal's dick, you would remember that."

"It was an accident," Tucker said.

Jordan raised a hand. "I'm not here to make an enemy of you. I think it's rather great to have you on the team. You exposed me as the whore of the school."

Delilah crossed her arms. "Well, she wasn't wrong."

"At least I didn't have to open my legs for my grades," Jordan said.

"Are we here to help each other or bitch each other out?" Emily asked. She knew that this wouldn't work if they were all going to use their dirt against each other.

"That's the point of the Revenged Queen. Bethany has created a culture where we are against each other. We are using our dirt to ruin each other. She thinks she was changing this world, but she wasn't. She ruined this damn school. We had a hierarchy, and she needs to fucking pay." Jordan slammed the desk.

"She believed she was doing something good for this school. She truly wanted you all to realize how horrible you all were acting," Tucker said.

"But she caused too much grief," Delilah said. She felt her heart in that moment. "She made me realize how horrible of a friend Danielle has been. People don't understand what it's like to lose a friend."

"I lost the girl I was in love with," Tucker said.

"No, she just deceived you. She knew damn well what she was doing from the beginning. She was a wallflower, and she was done playing in the shadows," Jordan said. "I'm done with people thinking they can get away with this shit." Jordan pulled out three files from her purse. "These are the three that will pay." She slid them across the table.

"Bethany and Danielle I get, but Susan?" Emily asked.

"She was part of The Marked Queen circle," Jordan said. She turned to Tucker. "You were one of the people I was planning to ruin, too."

"Don't worry, I still have the note."

"So, we can't trust him?" Delilah asked.

"No, it gives me more determination," Tucker said. He wanted to bring Bethany down, but he wasn't ready to give them the bomb just yet. He would give them the abortion truth, but he had to still process it himself.

"So, we know our targets. They will all be walking down the aisle in just one week. Let's give them a final farewell." Jordan looked at the files on the table. She knew how to expose Susan. She needed to find the final pieces on Bethany and Danielle. Danielle, you should have stopped The Marked Queen when you had a chance. You wouldn't have been on the chomping block.

Jordan pulled out her phone. "What are you doing?" Delilah asked.

"It seems our team is full. Why not let the kingdom know about us?" Jordan asked. Jordan, we agreed with you completely. You were right about your team being filled. We had no clue Tucker was your final member, but it was going to be such a shock for Bethany once it was all exposed. The clock was ticking, and the speeches were about to be given. It was going to get brutal. Jordan sent a mass text to the school, and it was delicious.

The Marked Queen, you have had your fun on the top. You made us all look like fools at prom. You believed that you didn't make enemies during your rule. Well, I'm here to show you that you created one angry bitch. Don't worry. You weren't the only one I wanted to see pay for their sins. People have backstabbed, betrayed, and lied to so many people. I'm here to make sure they get their just desserts. This queen is handing out the knives and determination to see their enemies suffer. It's time for someone else to sit on that throne, and it's going to be me- The Revenged Queen.

Chapter 29

Bethany read the text, and she knew The Revenged Queen was real. She hadn't heard from the bitch in a couple of days, and now she knew it was war. She had to make sure her secrets were safe behind closed doors. She wouldn't let her breakup with Tucker ruin her. Careful Bethany, you shouldn't quickly assume that Tucker was behind you. You had no clue Tucker was your enemy now.

She walked into the computer lab and Carter looked up to see Bethany walking in. He was surprised that Jordan was right. He didn't think it would take this long for her to come here, but he assumed it had to do with Jordan's text blast.

"My, my. I'm getting a visit from The Marked Queen." He leaned back. "How did I get so lucky?"

Bethany rolled her eyes. "You've always been an asshole, haven't you?" She slammed money on the table.

He leaned forward and grabbed it. "What's this for?"

"Carter, don't play stupid. We all know what that money is for. Your reputation has made you a name in getting things done."

"And your name has made it known not to trust you." Carter wanted to ruin Bethany's life after everything she did with Jasmine. He was happy to see she was doing so well in Barcelona. She looked tan, and he was still in love with her. Carter, you knew the bitch for less than a month. She was an ogre. Now, she was a beast with a tan.

She took a seat across from him. "Really? You're going to side with the popular kids? I thought you were on my side. You're one of the shadow people."

"But you went after Jasmine."

"Of course, you still have a thing for the daddy punching bag."

He grabbed the money and tossed it back at her. "I'm not going to help you."

"You really have a soft spot for her." She nodded. "I get what it's like to be in love with someone, and they want nothing to do with you."

"Are you talking about the public humiliation of Tucker dumping you earlier today?"

She laughed. "I shouldn't have been surprised that everyone was going to talk about it." She looked down. "My mom always talked about her time in high school. It was the best years of her life. I don't have any of those moments."

"Because you were a bitch to everyone," Carter said.

She looked at him. "I only became a bitch after I was bullied by the high society of this school. I only had Tucker. I thought if I proved that I was worth something then people would care about me. I created The Marked Queen to level the playing field."

"And how's that worked out for you?"

"People look at me. People know my name. I'm not some wallflower that people can walk all over. I think that's something I should be proud of."

Carter knew what it was like to be forgotten in this world. He was an outcast, and he had to give her respect for wanting to take down the high society. He knew how he felt when Jasmine rejected him for Calvin. He wasn't good enough because he didn't have social standing. Bethany made it where everyone could rise to the top.

He leaned forward and grabbed the money. "I don't like what you did to Jasmine, but I understand it. We weren't good enough for any of them, and we created ourselves to be useful to them."

"And we are still serving them." She shook her head. "I want to make sure I end up on top of something by the end of the year."

"What do you need me to do?" he asked.

"I need you to hack into the school and change my grades. I got so focused on making sure I took down those hoes, that I slipped up. I need to be valedictorian by the end of the year."

"You mean next week?"

"Yes."

"Haven't they already announced who is going to be valedictorian?"

"It's Johnson Prep. I got away with publicly humiliating people at prom. I thought there might still be a chance you can make me end up on top." She stood up. "Oh, and make sure my competition's grades somehow go down." She walked to the door.

"You really care about this, don't you?" Carter asked.

"I didn't have parties, football games, or even stupid sex with random guys. All I have is my grades. It was made clear that even though I was The Marked Queen, that I was nothing."

"How can I trust you?"

"I just gave you a secret of mine, and I have a secret on you. Mutual destruction."

"Why should I help you? The Marked Queen was a cruel person."

"Because I'm nothing like that persona. I only use her for the royals." She walked out of the room with that. Bethany, you couldn't lie to us. We all knew that The Marked Queen was exactly who you were. We hoped for your sake it didn't bite you in the ass.

Chapter 30

"Hey Danielle," Dan said. He was trying to be on his best behavior. He had been taking the time to think about how much he regretted letting his judgment ruin their relationship.

She slapped him across the face. "Hey, Dan."

"What the fuck?"

She crossed her arms. "Did you really think I was going to be civil with you after you decided to tell my mom about my online activities?"

"I thought she needed to know. I'm worried about you."

Dan, you really needed to give it a rest. You were a boring guy, and she deserved to be with someone who wasn't a sheltered asshole.

"Dan, I haven't needed you to worry about me," she said, then paused and thought about it. "Since you thought I wasn't the girl you fell in love with."

"But you came back to me." Dan thought they could make this work between them.

"No. You decided to be this social justice douche. I'm living my life, and you just judge it. Let's face it Dan, we were never meant to be together."

"Because you never could accept that you belong to this world."

Danielle shook her head. "No, I could never be a part of your world. You continued to make me believe I didn't have substance."

"You all have backstabbed each other to keep your secrets safe. Did prom just leave your memory?"

"No, because now I am free of my secrets. People know I'm poor, and my life didn't change much. Now I have to deal with my mother and ex-boyfriend attacking me for every decision I make."

"You deserve better than what you're doing."

"Now who's not accepting realty. You and my mother want me to be this moral princess, when I'm nowhere near that. I destroyed my best friend's reputation. I was a horrible to so many of my classmates. But I'm not going to be an after school special type of girl. I'm the bitch that breaks hearts, steals boyfriends, and satisfies boys wildest dirtiest dream."

"I'm so ashamed of you." Dan looked at Danielle. "Why aren't you achieving going to fashion school? Why aren't you sewing anymore?"

"What do you think I do with the cash I make from that website?"

"Buy designer clothes?" He assumed that was why she joined up.

"I'm saving up for college. I actually still make my own clothes." She showed him the dress she was wearing. "I made this a couple of days ago. I guess you think so little of me. You're a trailer park asshole. And I'm the vapid spoiled airhead. We really thought we could work out? Try again."

"Let's put our egos to the side. Let's work on us." Dan grabbed her hands. "I love you."

She laughed. "Fuck letting go of my ego. I'm enjoying the woman I'm becoming." She ripped her hands out of his. "I don't have to listen to trash like you anymore." She turned to walk away from him.

"I'll never stop loving you."

She turned to look at him. "Well duh. I'm the one that got away. You're just the first guy of many assholes that I'll end up dating. Have fun jerking off to me while you drink your pain away." She waved him out and walked away.

Bravo Danielle, you really knew how to leave him with a bruised ego. We couldn't have wanted this more. You needed to dump his annoying ass. We wished you didn't give up your dad's money, but we did enjoy you stripping and escorting more. Hope you keep this confidence when the Revenged Queen came for your ass.

****

"I'll be right with you," Jordan said, kissing the random guy on the lips. She had gone out again with Calvin. She felt like she was on a high right now. She had shown the world The Revenged Queen, she forgot everything about Shane, and she was becoming the bitch she always wanted to be. Careful Jordan, you might feel like you are flying high, but we had a feeling it was all bullshit. You better be prepared for a crash landing.

Val walked out of her room to see Jordan kissing the stranger on the lips and showing him where to go. Jordan turned to see her sister staring at her. "Another boy?" Val asked.

Jordan crossed her arms. "Do you have a problem with it?"

Val took the lollipop out of her mouth. "I think you're making some dangerous decisions lately, and I'm worried about you."

"You don't have to worry about little ole' me. I'm just having some fun." Jordan didn't need to hear a speech from her sister. She was finally getting back into a good place.

"Really? That's the fourth guy you've brought home this week alone."

"I'm surprised you've been home that much. I should give you a round of applause."

"You know that I have things going on. I'm reconnecting with some friends since I got back from college," Val said.

Jordan laughed. "You mean, doing a shit ton of drugs. Yes, I remember all about your parties when you were still going to Johnson Prep."

"Please, you were waiting for the day I left for you to take over."

Jordan nodded. "Yes, but you made sure to lock me in my room like I was some freak."

"I didn't need my sister coming off as a social climber."

Jordan got into Val's face. "You either hate that I've had better parties or that all your guy friends were so eager to fuck me."

"Yes, I'm proud that my sister became a whore." Val leaned forward. "Maybe you did deserve to get raped."

Jordan went to slap her, but Val grabbed her hand. "You fucking bitch," Jordan said. She felt so much rage for her sister in that moment. She had no right to bring up what happened with her.

"That's what men are going to say when it gets out what happened. That's what he thought when he fucking raped you." Val wanted her sister to understand what she was doing. She knew in her heart her sister didn't deserve what happened, but she needed to learn from it.

"That doesn't mean you get to rub it in my face. I'm trying to forget about it."

"By sleeping around? How is that working out for you?" Val asked.

"It's fine. I'm having the time of my life. I don't need you coming over here and attacking me for shit when you have no clue what's going on."

"Do any of your friends know?" Val asked. She was worried her sister had no one to go to. She knew her parents were never around, so that was a useless place to look for comfort.

Jordan laughed. "We're the Caraway sisters. We don't do friendship."

Val looked at her with a worried expression. "I don't believe that for a second. You could go to any of your friends, and they would be there for you. Emily?"

"Emily is currently dealing with her own shit."

"Everyone is dealing with their own shit. It doesn't mean she can't be there for you."

"Doesn't it? No one wants to be the needy person."

You were raped!" Val screamed.

"Do you want to scream that louder?" Jordan asked. "I get that you love sucking lollipops, but I prefer sucking cock."

"Jordan, you need to talk to someone other than me. You have friends in that school. You can go after that prick."

"You don't get it." Jordan looked at Val, and she had no clue how her sister could be this naïve. "Nothing will ever happen with Shane. He raped me, and he is going to get away with it. You need to drop it."

"But you're getting revenge on other girls that did wrong on you. Why not him?"

"Because it's easier to go after a bitch than a rich white male." She turned, because she was done with this conversation. She knew her sister was trying to make her stand up for herself, but she knew it was a useless fight. She would go after the girls that put her in that situation. Shane was a vile human being, but he wasn't the one that gave her that label. He wasn't the one that made her be looked at like less than a human.

Jordan walked into the room to please the man that had been waiting for her. She fooled around with him thinking about the reality of everything. She had no friends, she was raped, and people would continue to look at her like she was a slut. She had no one she could really count on. The popular girl with the loser self-esteem. It wasn't like we hadn't seen that time and again. We wished Johnson Prep was a better place. We prayed they would find common ground and people would truly connect with that. This wasn't a Hallmark movie, it was more of a horror one. We wanted a blowout, and Jordan, you had no clue you were about to deliver. Too bad for you, no one was going to be there for you once someone attacked you.

Chapter 31

"What's a pretty girl like you doing alone in a bar like this?" Richard asked, while taking a seat next to Delilah.

Delilah laughed and touched his arm. She wanted to play coy with him. She wanted to celebrate the release of The Revenged Queen to the world. She was disappointed in the fact that Danielle didn't seem worried when she read the text. She thought she would want to keep her secrets safe. Delilah, if you only knew what skeletons the bitch had in her closet.

"I was just waiting for a man to come join me." She leaned forward. "Do you know any?"

He laughed. "I might know a few, but I want you all to myself."

"Who says you can have me?" Delilah enjoyed this back and forth. She hadn't found men her age to be mentally stimulating. Delilah, weren't you the one that was fucking your principal to get better grades? Aren't you still the same bitch that will barely graduate high school? We wouldn't call it mental stimulation, because you were practically brain dead.

"You were the one that called me. I think you could say that I have on good authority you're into me."

She took a sip of her drink. She liked looking into his eyes. "I guess you do have a point. It amazes me that you're still single."

He shrugged. "Recently divorced can do that for you. My best friend and I both found ourselves being left by our wives. We wanted to meet younger girls."

"To feel better about yourselves?" Delilah knew the game all older men were playing when they met young girls.

"Is it that obvious?" he asked.

She shrugged. "A bit. So, is it working?"

"I feel my way is a bit more normal. My best friend is taking a more interesting path." Richard, you didn't need to downplay what your best friend was doing. We would all soon find out his dirty secret. How this city had such a small world feel to it was amazing.

She touched his leg. "It's good that you're getting out there. I like a man with confidence."

He chuckled. "It's good that a pretty girl like you wants anything to do with me." He paused as he took a drink. "What do you study?"

She knew that she needed to play up that she was in college. Delilah, you shouldn't worry too much. He would get his erection once he found out your long list of daddy issues.

"I'm studying creative writing. I want to be an author."

Richard thought it was a silly idea for her to do it. He chuckled. "A girl as pretty as you. Don't you think that's a bit out of your wheelhouse?" he asked.

"What does that mean?"

"Do you think you're smart enough for it?" he asked.

She thought she was finally done being told she was some dumb bitch. "I'm actually a finalist in a writing contest right now."

"Did you have someone help you write it?"

"Why does it seem shocking a woman can be a writer?"

"I believe women can be writers," Richard said. "Some of my favorite writers were women." He just didn't think this girl had it in her. "I just don't see you being a writer."

"Is it because of my looks?"

Zachary Ryan

He placed a hand on her leg. "Why are you trying to start a fight with me? All I was saying is that I never could see you being a writer."

"My parents are writers, and they raised me to be one."

"So, they're proud of you?"

Proud was a strong word. We would go with disappointed, ashamed, angry, and disgusted. "There are some ups and downs in our relationship right now." She looked down. She thought about her last conversation with her father. She truly believed that they would get back on the same page. She wanted her father back, and she didn't know if she would.

Richard noticed that she was a little down. This was your moment to fix the mess you just made for yourself. "I would love to read some of your work. You seem passionate about it."

Delilah's spirits rose immediately. She knew her other go to person was Mr. Rozengota. They hadn't been on speaking terms since her scandal came out. "Thank you. That would mean a lot to me."

"What are you working on right now?" he asked.

Delilah opened her mouth, but she couldn't think of anything. She had been so focused on The Revenged Queen that she hasn't written anything. She wanted to believe she was producing something great. It made her feel empty inside, because maybe she was only this stupid vapid girl. It was the worst when the girl finally figured out her true place in the world. "I'm working on a girl getting revenge on her best friend."

"It sounds dramatic. Is it based on true events?"

Delilah, you should have told him the truth. We wouldn't hold it against you. "There are some things that could be considered non-fiction."

Richard leaned in closer. "Why don't you tell me more? I would love to hear all about your creative process." He ran his fingers up her leg.

She knew what he was doing, and she felt like she would give it to him. She hadn't been with a man since Flynn, and she wanted to get that stench off her. "Why don't we cut the small talk and grab a hotel." She leaned in closer to him. "I think you've earned a little pleasure."

He closed the gap between them, and they began to kiss. She wanted this to be something true. He might have called her a dumb bimbo, but she would prove to him that she was something more than a whore.

Delilah, you should have taken the Jordan approach. She accepted she was nothing more than a cum rag. We didn't think you were a whore. We just appreciated you being a dumb bitch. You might have wanted to prove to people over and over again that you were someone special, but you still aren't. You tried it with your writing, but you were used. You tried with friendship, and you were backstabbed. It is all rather comical if you asked us.

"Why don't we get out of here? I'll book us a hotel upstairs," he suggested.

She leaned forward and kissed him on the lips. "Why do you think I wanted us to meet at a hotel?" She winked.

They ended up getting a hotel room. They had boring sex where he only lasted a couple of minutes. He apologized, and he started to get upset about how embarrassed he was. Delilah stroked his ego, because she didn't want this guy to run away from her. It was rather pedestrian if we had to comment on it all.

The only thing that made this moment different was how she laid there awake thinking about her life. Delilah truly felt like she had nothing going her way. She turned to Richard, who was snoring and dreaming of his ex-wife, and she thought about how she hadn't been writing lately. She was worried her anger with Danielle made her lose what was so special about her.

Delilah, we know who you were, and we could tell you right now. The only problem is you won't like our answer. You did lose your way with The Revenged Queen, and acknowledged that she had nothing else to look forward to. The real shit truth was that you had no one else to bounce off of. It was the true tragedy of Johnson Prep, no one had anyone in their corner. It was why they were all so fucked up, but it wouldn't be a salacious read without some misery.

Chapter 32

"How are you feeling about everything?" Emily asked.

Tucker and Emily were curled up in his bed. There hadn't had any sexy time since they both wanted to get to know each other. Emily, you should have sex with him sooner. You would learn why Bethany was such a frigid bitch.

"I don't know." He got out of bed. "We all saw how bad The Marked Queen was. Don't you think The Revenged Queen will be worse?"

"We are only going after three people."

"Susan doesn't deserve to get picked on. If we tell people about her mental breakdown, then that's going below the belt."

"But exposing child abuse, alcoholism, and eating disorders are okay?" Emily got out of the bed.

"Susan was trying to get Jasmine to humble herself and realize she had a real friend, when she was obviously going through stuff."

"And you're doing the same thing by being with us?"

"So, shouldn't I be getting exposed?"

Emily shrugged. "I don't know. All I know is that Jordan wants to go after the bitch." Emily leaned against the headboard. "I think she truly needs this. I can tell Jordan's been through a lot."

"Are you worried about her?" Tucker asked.

Emily looked away from him. She could tell her emotions were getting the best of her. "When that story broke, I could see a part of her falling apart. She doesn't have a lot of people in her corner. Her parents are never home, so she never really got what it meant to be comforted by people."

"But she has you."

"If you could consider that. Tucker, I'm not someone people easily trust. You can see that all over people's face, even my friends."

"Why's that?"

"After Matthew, I knew that I couldn't be strong for people. I was a fool to believe I could for Andrew, but it failed." She wanted to believe that she had the strength to keep going forward, but she wasn't so sure. She had Mathew and Andrew on her mind. She had received a letter from Andrew, but she hadn't been able to bring herself to open it yet.

Tucker thought about his next response, choosing his words carefully. "You've been there for me with everything about Elizabeth."

Has she though? Does she know you still scream yourself awake from nightmares about her? Or, have you told her how Elizabeth has been communicating with you?

"I think I got lucky with you. I make things worse."

"So, this is your way of being there for Jordan?" Tucker asked.

"In so many ways yes." Emily looked at Tucker. She thought about Andrew, remembering being bitch slapped by him at prom. She knew they were friends. "How could you do that to Andrew?"

Tucker knew that eventually this conversation would happen. He had felt guilty for what he did to Andrew. He was hurt that he wasn't hanging out with him, and he wanted to expose his dirty secrets. "I wanted someone to look more messed up than I did."

"He was your friend."

"And you were his girlfriend. How would he feel knowing we're together?" Tucker asked.

"I didn't expose his secrets for the world."

"But you kept getting him drunk. You had to admit something was up."

"I thought something was strange when I met up with him in the Bronx. He told me it was a group to help him with his paper. He and this woman got into an argument. He said they were arguing over the topic of his paper, but it seemed deeper than that."

"You decided not to pry."

"You didn't do much prying yourself or worrying after he pushed you away," Emily said. She didn't want to have an argument with Tucker. "I thought we agreed not to judge each other."

"It's not judging when we both fucked up with him."

"Do you regret it?" Emily asked.

"I only regret it because I felt like nothing has changed."

"How so?"

"Bethany has now become a bitch, and now were sitting here trying to take her down. Is this how it's always going to be?"

"Tucker, you graduate next week. I don't see it as being an issue. You're almost out of here." She turned to look at the files on his table. "Are these part of your final portfolio? She saw one stack that she wasn't sure she had seen before. "What are these?"

Tucker realized what she was going after. "Those are private." He grabbed them out of her hand.

Emily wanted to pry, but she wasn't going to. "Ok, so what do we do?" she asked. She wanted to know how they were supposed to move forward with this. She felt excited to find someone that was open about their struggles, and she wanted to see where it was going.

Emily, you had no clue what excitement waited for you. We hoped you had a strong back bone, but we doubted you would be on the straight and narrow for long.

"About?" he asked.

She kissed him on the lips. "Us."

"Honestly, I think we should take it slow. We don't define it."

Tucker, you could have told her the truth. You were just using her for a rebound. You still loved Bethany, and you regretted kissing Emily.

Emily thought that was the appropriate approach. Emily and Tucker, you both couldn't fool us. You both weren't over your exes. You were trying to find comfort in each other. Too bad for you, the pain of your past was about to ruin your present. Hoped you both could cope, because we had a fucking feeling both of you would fail spectacularly.

****

Danielle took a line of coke while her and Christian were in the limo together. She had just left her date with a new client. He wanted her to come on a double date with him tomorrow night. He wanted to show her off, and he was paying her five hundred dollars to do it.

Christian leaned forward and started to kiss her neck. "You're driving me crazy."

She laughed as she pushed him off her. "You really think some cheesy lines are going to get me going?"

He fixed his suit. He ran his fingers through his hair. "You don't want to play with me?"

She pulled out a compact mirror. She grabbed her red lipstick and fixed her make-up. "I never once said I wouldn't play around with you," she chuckled. "Besides, it's more fun teasing you."

"So, what do you plan on doing with all your money?" Christian asked, changing the subject.

"Why? Are you asking me to invest in your business, or something?" she asked.

He shrugged. "I wouldn't mind having a woman on the team. I don't have that 'female touch' to make sure the girls feel comfortable."

"And because you've slept with them all."

"That's not true," Christian said. He had smarts when it came to his business. He also didn't find any of the girls as alluring as Danielle. He craved more of her. He wanted to take that dress off and pleasure her right then.

Danielle could see Christian trying to seduce her. She knew it was working, because she was ready to run her fingers through his hair. She wanted to rip that suit off his perfectly muscular body. She craved the rough, dirty, immoral sex she knew he was capable of.

"You don't need to worry. I believe you," she said. She sat back with a glass of champagne.

Christian looked at her for a moment. He remembered the girl she was when they first met. "You seem fearless now."

She turned to look at him. "How so?"

"You were so worried about doing the right or wrong thing. You wanted to be a good person, and now, you don't give a rat's ass if you keep your wings," he said. He enjoyed this side of her the most. He didn't care for the journey of self-improvement.

"My mother knows now."

"And?"

"And I don't care anymore. I helped her pay off back rent. I've saved money to go to college. I'm making dreams and moves for myself." She took a sip of her champagne. "I'm going to be someone someday. I'll be someone better than The Marked Queen."

"You miss your kingdom," he said. Christian figured it out now. "You had it all, and it was taken away from you," he chuckled.

"That bitch told the world that I was some common trash, my mother told me to be proud of it, and my boyfriend wanted me to stay that way forever. Isn't that just cruel?"

"Because you would have to be wholesome?"

She shook her head. She leaned forward. "I would have to be forgettable." She took another line of coke. "Don't you get it? I was powerful there."

Christian loved her anger in this moment. He could feel his blood rushing to his waist. "Do you want it all back?"

She waved him off. "That's child's play. I have more power now than I did then." Danielle saw the text from The Revenged Queen. She thought it was cute, but she wasn't really stressed about the new girl uncovering her dirty secrets. She didn't care if it happened or not.

"I thought The Marked Queen wasn't going to be dethroned?"

"You care about what happens at Johnson Prep?" she asked.

"I hear about the drama that goes on there. Your gossip is very popular in the city."

Danielle rolled her eyes. "The modern-day Gossip Girl. How cute."

"I think she was way more ruthless with her scandals than Gossip Girl," he said.

She looked Christian straight in the eyes. "The Revenged Queen can come out with any dirt she wants on me. I don't care."

"Good. Now that I know you're above it all, I have a business proposal for you." He knew his views and her views would go up if they did videos together. "Why not partner up on some videos together? You are the hottest girl on the site, and I'm the hottest male. Everyone would pay great money to see us collaborate together."

Danielle scooched over to be closer to him. "Have fun for the world's delight?" she asked.

He nodded. He took a sip of his drink. "I'm trying to make money here, and I know you are too." He was planning to run away for six months. He needed to get out of this town, and he was hoping to convince Danielle to take over his business while he was gone.

She looked at him. "Fine, but if we're going to let the world in on our fun, I want to do it solo first." She grabbed his tie and pulled him toward her. Their lips crushed together. Christian finally was going to get his prize, and he wasn't going to let her get away.

He slid down the seat as she got on top of him. He began to pleasure her body as she took off his clothes. Danielle, you were our fucking hero. We were jealous you got to seduce such a fine piece of ass. Christian wasn't holding back when he pounded into Danielle. Danielle clawed the back of Christian's back. Danielle, weren't you glad you dumped that boyfriend of yours? Boys and girls, this was how you fucked like sluts. Christian took control of her, and she was willing. They steamed up those windows and stained those seats. Their sexual experience was filled with pleasure and fueled by coke. Hoped it continued, because the sight of Christian naked left all of us having a wet spot in our underwear.

****

"I didn't see why we needed to meet at your house for this," Jordan said, walking into Alassane's house.

Alassane laughed. "I thought we could get to know each other." He led her to the kitchen and dining room area. "You can put your stuff here and make yourself at home. Do you want anything to drink?" he asked.

Jordan dropped her bags and books on the table. She followed him into the kitchen. She noticed there was something cooking on the stove, but she assumed it was family dinner later. "You don't have to be so nice to me."

He grabbed two waters out of the fridge. He handed her one. "Why not?"

"You graduate in a couple of days. This project is due tomorrow. I'm just going to be some blimp on your radar."

"I don't know. I feel like you're someone interesting." He leaned against the counter. "Why do you find it weird people being nice to you?" he asked.

"I just want to know if someone is using me," Jordan said.

Aw Jordan, it must have sucked to know that people were only interested in using you for your house, alcohol, and your body. You really didn't have anyone in your corner, did you?

He went over to the stove to check on the chicken parmesan. "I have nothing to gain from you. Yeah, you had a lot of great parties, but people didn't really notice me there. If I wanted to sleep with you, I think all those chances went out the window after you thought I was gay."

Jordan chuckled. "You haven't eye fucked me since I've met you."

He turned to look at her. "Sorry, you're not my type."

"I'm everyone's type, minus Calvin's." Jordan looked at Alassane. She had to admit she would watch a porn of them doing it.

Jordan, we were right there with you. Calvin would probably do it too, but he was busy making sure he wasn't too sick.

He pulled the chicken parmesan out of the oven and placed it on the stove. He turned to look at her. "And once again, I don't do dudes." He had a smile on his face.

"Did you cook dinner for your family?" he asked.

"My parents have a friend's birthday dinner tonight, and my brother is on some camping trip." He grabbed two plates out of the cabinet. "This is for us."

"Wait? You cooked us a meal?" she asked.

He could tell that she was freaking out. "I'm not interested in you. I wanted to cook you a meal. I wanted to be nice."

She shook her head. "No one cooks me a meal to be nice."

Alassane felt sorry for Jordan in that moment. "Do you not have any true friends? You always have so many people at your house. Everyone knows who Jordan Caraway is."

She raised a hand. "I need to use your bathroom."

Alassane wanted to pry, but he didn't want to cause anymore drama. "It's through those doors to the left. I'll get this ready." Alassane always cooked for his friends. It was one of the things he enjoyed doing. How cute was Alassane? Did you cook for Flynn when he was destroying Delilah's confidence?

Jordan walked into the bathroom. She felt her whole body plagued with nerves. She didn't get why she was freaking out about this. It was just a meal. It felt like a marriage proposal, and she barely knew the guy. She splashed water in her face.

"Do you think you deserve nice things? You are, after all, trash," Shane said.

Jordan looked up to see Shane's smug smile. "I do deserve good things in my life."

He laughed. "How do I not believe you? It's okay. Come on, Jordan. You can't fool me with your bullshit. You're a bitch. You are about to ruin so many girls' lives with their secrets."

"Because they ruined mine."

He shook his hand. "We all know you did that on your own."

"You did after all sleep with multiple sports teams. I just was reporting on it," Bethany said, standing behind Jordan.

Jordan turned to look at Bethany. "Fuck you, bitch." She leaned against the door staring at them both.

"Let's face it, Jordan. Your only friend is Emily. We all know how much of a train wreck she can be. You're having a panic attack because a guy cooked you a meal and is being friendly toward you," Bethany said.

Shane turned to look at Bethany. "She's only used to a guy undressing her."

"But he doesn't want anything to do with her," Bethany said.

Shane laughed again. "Because he knows how used up she is. Face it, Jordan. Everyone has had a piece of you, and people are over used goods."

Bethany shook her head. "You're The Revenged Queen coming for my crown." She made a disapproval look. "You will have no one in your corner to defend you when the chips fall." Bethany leaned forward. "You're nothing more than a party girl that any guy can have their way with. It was why you didn't come forward about Shane. You've had more people enter you than a local Starbucks."

"I didn't get dumped in front of the whole school." Jordan shot back hoping it would offend Bethany.

Bethany faked hurt. "Was that the best you could do? Maybe you should have been The Pathetic Queen unlike Jasmine. At least I had a boyfriend who was proud to stand by myside, do you?"

"She couldn't even get a guy to sleep with her because they were afraid they were going to get something from her."

"But you raped me." Jordan looked at Shane.

He shrugged. "I still didn't brag to my friends about you because you're a dirty secret. Everyone who has fucked you feels ashamed. Has anyone called you back after they've slept with you?"

Bethany turned to look at Shane. "Alassane is the only guy to even talk to her."

"But he's not interested." They both laughed right in her face.

Jordan felt the tears falling down her face. She opened the door and ran out of the room. Alassane could tell that something was wrong. "Are you okay?"

Zachary Ryan

Jordan saw the worry on his face. She grabbed her purse and books. "I need to go. Sorry." She left, hoping to never have to face Alassane. She had Shane and Bethany's words stuck in her heart. They were right. No one has ever really gotten to know her, and she knew that there was nothing to enjoy once the alcohol wore off. Jordan, there must be a lot going on in your head if a guy making you dinner, had you having a mental breakdown. You had better get your shit together, because we needed The Revenged Queen to go after some bitches, not cry in the corner like some Sarah McLachlan shelter dog.

Chapter 33

"Aman, you okay?" Calvin asked. He didn't really want to have a conversation with Aman, but he saw how destroyed he looked standing at his locker.

Aman turned and smiled at Calvin. "I'll be fine. I'm just going through some shit."

Calvin wanted to walk away, but his heart wanted to know if he was going to be okay. He reached out and squeezed his hand. "You know I'm here for you," Calvin said with a smile.

"Thank you." Aman wanted to break down to him right there, but he didn't know how he could. He was trying to process that Sana had left him. Sana accused him of being in love with Calvin. He wasn't over him, and he knew he never would be able to walk away from him.

Aman saw Calvin begin to walk away. "Calvin."

Calvin turned. "Yeah?"

"Can we talk by the bleachers?" Aman asked.

Calvin smiled. "Sure."

They walked to their old hiding spot. They sat in silence for a couple of minutes, and Calvin didn't know if he was supposed to say anything. He was trying to figure out if he should just get up and leave. "I never meant to hurt you. I thought I was doing the right thing."

"What?"

Aman and Calvin turned to look at each other. "Calvin, I'm still in love with you."

"What about Sana?"

"Sana knows the truth. I think she always knew. We didn't have sex a lot, there was never conversations that made us connect, and she could never hold a light to you." Aman wanted to avoid the truth, but it was staring him right in the face.

Calvin turned to look away from him. "My life hasn't been easier without you in it. I prayed that I would forget you." He thought about Terrell. "I thought if I met someone else, that I'd be able to move past you."

"But?"

"I still couldn't find someone that I connected with more than you. I see you in the halls, and I still feel my stomach turn into knots. I look at photos of us, and I wish we could go back to how we were." Calvin looked at Aman. "I never stopped loving you."

"And no one compares to you." Aman couldn't do it anymore. He needed Calvin; he craved his touch. He grabbed Calvin's shirt and pulled him in for a kiss.

Calvin wanted to protest it, but it felt so good to have Aman's lips on his again. He craved his touch. Calvin, you finally found someone who kisses you with love. It was brutal to know that you were moving backwards, not forwards.

Calvin's brain caught up to him. "Aman, we can't be doing this in public."

"Why not?" Aman asked.

Aman, you were such a frightened kitty when it came to kissing Calvin in public, now you were all over him. Sana, you must have hated yourself right now. You made a closet gay want to go public.

"Because we are in public. What if your parents found out?" Calvin asked.

Aman cupped Calvin's face in his hands. "I don't care about them right now. All I want to worry about is you. We've wanted this for weeks now. Calvin, I've missed you. My life hasn't been the same without you. I need you back."

Calvin looked into Aman's eyes, and he wanted to believe everything that he was saying. He would never deny the rush he felt having Aman in his arms. He would never admit that this made him feel more complete. "I love you, Aman."

"I love you too, Calvin." Aman leaned forward again and kissed him. They didn't care if anyone found out about their little activity in the dug-out. We all were curious if this was a quick lapse of judgment for Aman.

Calvin, we prayed you didn't think too much into it. We didn't want you to go back into that prison of the closet without fully thinking it out. We also hoped you told Aman about your doctor visit in the next couple of days. We wouldn't want him to catch anything from you without being fully aware. It looked like our favorite love birds were finally getting back together, but we were all betting it wouldn't last. Boys and girls, this was why you never went back to an ex. It started out full of promise, and it ended up hurting like a bitch when it was over, like the pain Calvin felt when he peed.

Chapter 34

Danielle, we were curious how you were going to get yourself out of this one. You were facing the one person that wanted to destroy you the most. What a small world it was that your client was best friends with Delilah's new boyfriend. We would have called it coincidence, but we felt like this was fate all along.

"So, this is your best friend that had different ways of finding dates?" Delilah whispered into Richard's ear.

"He found her on some fetish website, and they've bonded since," Richard said.

Delilah smiled. "Interesting." Delilah took a sip of her drink. "I'm Delilah." She reached across the table.

Danielle knew she was caught, and she didn't know how she was going to get out of this one. "Danielle."

"It's so nice to meet you."

Danielle needed a moment alone. She felt like her walls were caving in, and she had to get out of there. She turned to her date as he was talking to his best friend. "I need to use the lady's room. I'll be right back." Danielle didn't wait for a response. She got up and walked away.

She walked into the bathroom and took in a shaky breath. She wanted to run away from this date, but Christian told her he was paying her five hundred dollars. She couldn't run away from the money. She was starting to save for college, and she needed to get the hell out of New York.

Danielle saw Delilah walk in. "I was wondering how much it would cost me to get a night alone with you."

Danielle looked at her. "I didn't know you were going lesbian? It makes sense since men our age don't find you appealing. It must be hard knowing daddy isn't around anymore, and I'm not talking about your father."

Delilah laughed. "You think people are going to care that I'm sleeping with an older man?" She walked over and washed her hands. "I slept with our principal. That's more scandalous than this." She walked over and grabbed a napkin to wipe her hands. "You being an escort is way more interesting, in my opinion."

"What are you going to do, run to The Revenged Queen and tell her?" Danielle asked.

Delilah could have told her right then that she was part of the queen team. "I don't know. Maybe I'll hold this against you as blackmail."

"Why?"

"Because I'm one bitter bitch."

Danielle rolled her eyes. "You're still not over that. I don't know how many more times I need to apologize to you. I made a mistake, and I'll have to live with it."

"But you don't care that you did it."

"Honestly, I've had a lot more shit on my mind. I only went into this fucking business because I was about to lose my damn home."

"The mighty Danielle has fallen," Delilah said. She was worried for her friend. She never thought she would see her this low. "Your father isn't helping anymore?"

"He stopped after I gave back the money and decided to be a good person. This was before my mom told me that she was couple of months late on rent. We were about to get evicted because of it."

"And you found this? How?" Delilah was more curious about it.

Zachary Ryan

Danielle leaned against the counter. "We aren't friends. You made that very clear to me."

Delilah reached out and squeezed her hand. "I hate you so much right now, but we've been friends since we were little. I thought I was in the same league as Calvin, and it hurt when I found out that I wasn't." Delilah paused. "It doesn't mean that I don't still care about you."

Danielle could see the sincerity in her eyes. She knew Delilah wasn't a good actress. "I'm sorry for what I did. I didn't mean to expose your secrets, but I was trying to keep some standing." She looked at Delilah. "I got into this because I needed the money. I'm staying because I crave the attention. Ever since The Marked Queen took my title, I haven't had anyone really look at more or want me. I'm having men pay hundreds of dollars because they find me desirable."

Delilah sat next to Danielle. "I haven't been writing. I'm only with this guy because it's nice to have someone look at me as something of value."

Delilah, he was with you for your body, not your brains. We really wished you would learn that.

"So, things at home aren't great?" Danielle asked.

Delilah shrugged. "My mom won't speak to me since the principal scandal came out. My father is never around. I haven't found any form of inspiration, and I feel like I'm just lost."

"It seems everyone expects us to have it figured out."

Delilah leaned her head on Danielle's shoulder and closed her eyes. "And we're about to graduate in a matter of days."

"Can you believe we're finally here?"

Delilah and Danielle looked at each other. "We're finally leaving Johnson Prep. We're going on our own, and it scares me," Delilah said.

186

"But, maybe this can be the start of our friendship again?" Danielle asked.

Delilah nodded and smiled. They pulled each other into a hug, and it was nice to see these girls finally bond again. We hoped it lasted. "I need to fix my make up," Delilah said.

"I'll meet you out there." Danielle winked and walked out of the room.

Delilah's smile faded once the door closed. She pulled out her phone and texted Jordan. "

Delilah: *So, it looks like our former queen has been selling herself on the streets. Queen to tramp, it was quite the justification for her actions during prom. I have the dirt on Danielle, and I can't wait for it to be exposed at graduation.*

Delilah pressed send without a second thought.

It looked like Delilah was a better actress than we all thought. Danielle, you had really lost your touch. You should have known not to show all your cards to a spiteful bitch out for revenge. You knew there was a new queen on the loose, and you had no clue you just gave her exactly what she needed. You were about to get one final lesson before Johnson Prep kicked your cheap ass to the curb.

****

Bethany walked into the living room to see her mom looking at a yearbook. "Mom, what are you doing?" she asked.

Linda looked up at her daughter. "I guess I'm getting nostalgic." Linda patted for her daughter to come sit next to her.

Bethany rolled her eyes. She knew her mom was going down memory lane. She took a seat next to her. "Why are you looking at your yearbook?"

Linda flipped through the pages. "I can't believe you graduate high school in five days. It seems like yesterday I was bringing you home from the hospital." Linda paused. "You've had a lot of hardships in your life, and it's good that you're still my happy girl."

Bethany tried to ignore the pain she felt from knowing her father wasn't going to be with them when she graduated. Bethany's father died when she was a little girl. It was a mass shooting at his business firm, after an old co-worker got disgruntled. Bethany stopped on a page. It was her father and her mother in high school. "You both were so pretty."

Linda looked at the photo. She giggled. "Your father was quite the charmer back then. He was so popular, and he could have had any girl he wanted."

"Mom, you were head cheerleader. Of course he was going to go for you." The popular guy and girl of high school ended up having a reject of a daughter. We would like to call it irony, but Bethany deserved to be in the swamp with the rest of the filth.

Linda closed her eyes. "I remember going to all the parties with my best girlfriends. All the boys were all over us. We would stay up late, smoke, and our parents would be none the wiser to us."

Mom, you make it sound like you were raised in the 60's. Did you also drink malts and pray dad went steady with you?" Bethany asked.

Linda nudged her daughter. "I just wanted this for you. I want you to look back on your high school years with the same amount of fondness that I did."

"Mom, I decided to choose a future for myself. I thought going to parties, having useless friends, and mediocre boyfriends would distract me from achieving my goals." Bethany, you didn't need to lie to your mother. No one wanted you at their parties, you were too much of a cunt to have friends, and let's not forget you being dumped by a mouth breather in the middle of the cafeteria.

"But you missed out on so much of high school. The top grades, the awards, and the scholarships won't matter when it comes down to it." Linda wanted her daughter to see that she missed out on so many experiences by focusing too much on academics.

"Mom, I'm valedictorian. Aren't you proud of me for that?"

Linda patted her on the knee. "Yes, I would never diminish your accomplishments." She paused. "Is Tucker proud of you?"

Bethany thought that was an odd question to ask. "Why are you bringing him up?"

"I haven't seen him around lately."

"Mom, we are finishing up finals and projects. We only have two days left of school." Bethany didn't know how to feel. She had only two more days left of school before she said her goodbyes to that place for good. She still had to get her cap and gown, go through graduation rehearsal, and then graduate.

"I know, honey. I was right there with you. I know how stressful this can be for you both. You don't know if you're both going to last together, and you never want to hold each other back."

"Did dad hold you back?" Bethany asked.

Linda shook her head. "No, your father and I knew what we were doing long ago. We always had open communication. It's like you and Tucker." Yes Bethany, you had great communication with Tucker.

We couldn't have agreed with your mother more. You did tell him about the abortion, after the fact. He told you how he hated you, right to your face. You both knew how to make a relationship work... oh wait.

Bethany looked down at her mother's yearbook. "Yeah, Tucker and I do have a great relationship. I think we will be okay in the end." Bethany stood up. "I'm going to go to bed."

"No problem, sweetie." Linda closed the yearbook and stood up. "I better get some rest. I fly to Chicago tomorrow for some last-minute business. I'll be gone for a couple of days. It would be a good time to throw and end of the year party." Linda winked before she walked up the stairs.

Bethany stood there in her living room ready to cry. She wouldn't have these moments like her mother. She wanted to believe that she would be proud of her high school years, but she knew they were all a bust. She sucked up the feelings, and she had a new plan. She would leave Johnson Prep with one memory. She was going to improve herself, and she would throw an end of the year party to prove she wasn't a pathetic loser.

Bethany, you could try all you wanted. You knew the saying, you might paint lipstick on a loser, but it would still be a loser. You believed you were going to end up on top, but you were delusional. Your mom cried tears of joy when she thought of her high school years, would you?

****

Delilah walked into Mr. Rozengota's room to see Flynn packing up his stuff. He saw Delilah standing there. "I guess I should be bowing to you."

"What do you mean?" she asked.

He rolled her eyes. "I hate how naïve you are. You think you're this bad ass now, but you'll never be more than the slut that opened her mouth for the principal."

"And you'll always be known as the boy who was too arrogant to write on his own," she said. She wasn't going to let some stupid crush she had ruin her confidence.

"I told you over and over again that I did what I needed to get ahead."

She crossed her arms. "How well did that work for you?"

"You need to learn to let it go. You got your revenge on me. Why don't we call it a truce? I lost my scholarships because of it," Flynn said.

Flynn, you should have thought twice about stealing from a girl you thought was so naïve.

"I can't because I was falling in love with you. I really believed you gave me the confidence to write for this world. You took that away from me." Delilah felt so good getting this out to Flynn. She didn't realize how much she needed this.

"And you were a fool to believe any of it."

"Exactly. Which is why I have a wall up against all of you. You caused me to become this horrible person. I don't let anyone in."

He shook his head. "You're still the same weak girl. You just changed up the mask."

Delilah didn't want to believe him. She was stronger now. She wasn't going to let some stupid boy tell her otherwise. "I

191

wasn't weak enough to call you out on your bullshit. I won't let anyone walk all over me anymore."

He laughed. "At least I'm still writing, are you?" he asked. He noticed how during free write she stared blankly at a piece of paper. She had hit her peak, and she wasn't falling gracefully.

He didn't give her a chance to respond. He brushed past her. "He still can hold a grudge, can't he?" Mr. Rozengota asked.

She walked over and leaned against a desk. "It seems we all can't escape from our identifiers. If I recall, you still look at me differently," she said. She couldn't get the image of his expression on his face out of her mind.

Mr. Rozengota knew that he was disappointed in Delilah. He saw her as his own daughter, and for that he couldn't look at her the same. Mr. Rozengota, you should apply to be her actual father. We heard the position was currently occupied, but hopefully, she didn't get attached enough to show you how she enjoyed father-daughter time between the sheets.

"And I owe you an apology for that." He walked over and leaned against his desk. "I believe you have so much talent to share."

She chuckled softly. "I think that was a fairytale, and we both know it."

He handed her back her paper. "I don't think so. You won the scholarship," he said.

"What?" Delilah was stunned. She also forgot about the scholarship for a moment. She had been so wrapped up in her revenge that she forgot about how much she wanted this. "I never thought it would happen."

"They believe in the words that are written on those pages. Why don't you?" he asked.

She looked at him. "Because no one will ever believe that I'm more than a girl who is a dumb bimbo."

"Or an angry girl at that."

"What do you mean?" she asked.

"Delilah, I'm observant of you. I see how you behave toward some of your classmates."

"You also know what happened at prom," she said.

The faculty decided they would ignore the complete disaster that was prom. They thought it was better if the students figured it out themselves. What was with the adults in this city ignoring the recklessness of the children? They wouldn't figure it out, you would see at graduation. You were all so stupidly blind, but that was okay, because it made it more interesting for us.

"But it shouldn't hold this much control over you." He paused. "Where did this girl go?" He pointed to the paper.

"You mean, the one with so much self-doubt."

"But she had a good heart. Delilah, you haven't written anything. Tomorrow is your last day in this school, and you plan to go out as the angry girl."

Delilah thought about it for a minute. She was proud that this could be her legacy. She also remembered the many days she got laughed at or called a whore because of the scandal that came out only a couple of weeks ago. "It seems like a lifetime ago that I was this girl."

"Do you plan to get revenge on these horrible students?" he asked.

She looked at him. "Don't worry. I won't shoot up the school. I'm not a white male."

"I didn't think you had that much anger inside of you." He paused and reached over and touched her hand. "You have a lot of talent inside of you, and you need to realize that won't get you anywhere. Your last days in this school are here. Do you really want them to be bad ones?"

"I don't know," Delilah said. She looked down at this paper, and she wanted to go back to this girl.

Delilah, we didn't want you to be the stupid girl anymore. We enjoyed this new confident bitch. We prayed that you continued down this path, at least until you got your revenge. We wondered if you would be able to show your face after graduation? Could you live with yourself after ruining lives? Maybe you would be able to write yourself a new life because in a few short days, you wouldn't like this one.

Chapter 35

"What are you doing here?" Jordan asked, opening the door for Alassane.

Alassane could tell that Jordan was clearly drunk. She was standing there with a bottle of vodka, a ripped dress, and her mascara running down her face. Jordan, you really knew how to attract a guy, don't you? "You called me," Alassane said.

Jordan grabbed his phone. She looked at the missed calls and the texts messages she sent him. She didn't even remember texting him. "It was a mistake. You didn't need to come over."

Alassane stepped inside. He grabbed the bottle from her. "I think I should stay."

She started fighting for the bottle back. "I don't need your pity, love, or you caring just to get into my pants."

He placed the bottle on the table. "I'm not trying to sleep with you."

She grabbed her heart. "I should feel hurt." She touched his arms and ran her fingers down his torso. "Come on. You don't even want to see what all the rumors are about?" She got to his waist. "We don't need to tell anyone," she said with a wink.

He was starting to get uncomfortable. He really didn't like her like this. He stepped back a moment. "Jordan, you're drunk. I'm not going to take advantage of you."

She rolled her eyes. "It wouldn't be the first time a guy took advantage of me." She turned and walked toward the living room. She took a seat on the couch.

He followed her into the living room. "What do you mean by that?"

She grabbed the other bottle of liquor off the table. She was trying to black out for the night. She wanted to go out, but Calvin wasn't responding to her text. She didn't even know where her sister was. "Oh, you didn't hear. I was raped." She took a swig of the bottle. "But I shouldn't be surprised. I deserve it."

He walked over and sat next to her. "No one deserves to be raped," he said. Alassane didn't know what to feel or how to react in this moment. He wanted to protect this broken girl that was in front of him. He always thought Jordan had it all, but he was starting to realize that it was a façade.

She looked at him with a smile. She could tell in his conviction that he actually meant it. She curled up to him. She needed his comfort. "You're the first person that I've told, minus my sister."

He began to stroke her arm. "Why not?"

"Because I have no one to go to."

"I don't believe that. You're always surrounded by people. You're one of the most popular girls in the school."

"Haven't you seen any movies? The girl you think that has all the friends isn't the popular girl. The girl surrounded by people is probably the most lonely."

"I don't believe you. I think you've got someone you can turn to."

"It was why I freaked out at your house the other day. I've never had someone be so sweet to me." Jordan didn't look at him. "My nanny was the only one that comforted me. She would help me with homework, and she would listen to my stories. Val, my sister, and I adored her."

"What happened to her?"

Jordan shrugged. "We got older, and my parents didn't see the need for her. They also didn't realize how much we truly craved her affection." Jordan turned to look at Alassane. "My parents are always traveling for work, parties, vacations, and escaping the reality that they're parents." Jordan thought of Nanny May, and she wanted nothing more than to hear from her again. She remembered the day they said goodbye to her, and it still killed her.

"Are you and Val close?"

"As we can be. She has her own life, and she's trying to find her own comfort in this world. It's the curse of being a Caraway. You're surrounded by worshippers, but you don't have a foundation."

Alassane didn't know what else to say. He knew that it was wrong that she didn't really have anyone in her life. She lost all affection, and it made him understand why she freaked out the other day at his house. "You don't need to be the party girl anymore then," he said. He thought if she got rid of this persona, she could let people in.

"I created an atmosphere for everyone to escape their problems and be free even if it's only for a few hours. I believe if I submerged myself with people, then I could be someone I eventually liked." Jordan looked at Alassane again. "Do you know how heartbreaking it is that I'm surrounded by people, and they don't see the tears coming from behind the mask? My broken soul is forced together by drunken boys trying to get off who never have to acknowledge my existence again when the sun comes up."

It was then that Alassane saw the true Jordan, and he wanted nothing more than to be her friend. He wanted to see what was behind the mask, and make sure she knew she was never alone again. He pulled her close and kissed her on the cheek. "I'll be here for you. I'll be your foundation, and I'll make sure you never feel alone again."

Jordan closed her eyes to those promises. She drifted to sleep for the first time in the arms of someone that actually cared for her. Aw Jordan, you finally made a friend. We hoped he was still willing to protect you once he knew you were behind the destruction that would ruin graduation. You had better sleep tight, The Revenged Queen, because in a few short days the only words associated with you were going to be 'ruthless bitch.'

Chapter 36

Bethany, we were pleased that you finally got rid of your frigid bitch look. You walked the hallways of Johnson Prep with sex appeal. You wore the marked dress with attitude, you had new dirty blonde hair, and was that red lipstick instead of chapstick? The wallflower finally accepted that she was queen.

People were whispering as she walked by. "I'm having a party tomorrow night. It's the end of the year, and we should be celebrating, darlings," she said, while passing out invitations to her party. She took her mother's advice, and she was going to throw one last party before they all said their goodbyes to this school. She wanted to be known as someone other than a boring girl who seemed like she would be horrible in bed. Those were our words, not anyone else's.

She walked up to Danielle and handed her an invite. "Here. I'm having a party tomorrow night. You should come."

Danielle looked at the invite. She had plans with Christian tomorrow. They were going to try the whole threesome experience with a client. "You're trying to be the party girl I see. Shouldn't you stick to being a wallflower?"

Bethany crossed her arms. "Why? You're trying act like you're rich."

Danielle nodded. "It's nice that you're showing off your bitch side instead of keeping it hidden."

Bethany smiled. "Someone's got to show you bitches how it's done. I'm not ashamed of ruining people's lives."

Danielle turned to see Tucker and Emily getting cozy. "You might think you're loved by these minions, but even your boyfriend ran away from you."

Zachary Ryan

"I don't see you having one either."

Danielle laughed. "Have fun at the top." She placed the invite on Bethany's chest. "It's a bitch when you fall from grace." Danielle walked away from her. She was ready for tomorrow to be here. She was ready to never walk through these halls again.

Bethany ignored Danielle's comments. She wouldn't have her execution day. She was loved by the people. She knew The Revenged Queen was a nobody, and she shouldn't worry about it. It was quite adorable seeing this bitch walk the halls and assume everyone adored her. It would be a rude awakening when she was at the guillotine.

She walked up to Susan who was talking to some friends. She handed her an invite. "I thought you should know I'm having a party tomorrow night." She looked at who Susan was hanging out with. "You can invite them too, if you want."

Susan grabbed Bethany's hand and pulled her to the side. She had wanted to talk to her since The Revenged Queen's text went out. She had tried to keep a low profile, and Susan's new friends didn't care about the social hierarchy. Susan, that was because they were irrelevant, we didn't know their names, nor did we care.

"Aren't you worried about The Revenged Queen?"

Bethany rolled her eyes. She regretted bringing Susan into the mix. She gave her some good dirt, but she didn't need to deal with this uselessness. "Why are you so worried about some bitch that hasn't made herself known?"

"Maybe, because she's waiting for the perfect time to expose us, like graduation."

"She would take a move out of my book. You would think she'd be original."

Susan looked at Bethany. She couldn't believe how delusional she was being. "You really think you're invincible from all of this? We all have secrets we're trying to keep hidden."

Bethany laughed. "I've kept my shit together over the years. I've made sure that no one has blackmail on me." Bethany leaned forward. "You, on the other hand, might want to be very careful."

Susan got nervous. "What does that mean?"

"Susan, we've all seen the tape."

"What?" Susan was praying Bethany wasn't talking about her meltdown. She knew The Revenged Queen found out, but she didn't know Bethany discovered it.

Bethany pulled out her phone and went to a video. It was Susan drunk trying to seduce Eddie. "I think you could have done better than Eddie, but we all make our choices."

Susan sighed a little bit. She blushed. "I didn't know Eddie had a girlfriend."

"Veronica was pissed, but she deserves it. She thinks she's better than everyone because she's a cheerleader."

Susan looked down at the invite. "Thank you, I'll tell my friends."

Bethany leaned forward and kissed her on the cheek. "Good. I'm going to prove to these pathetic ants that I'm the queen of this school. People will remember my name by the end of this."

Bethany went around and passed out invites to everyone. She kissed them all on the cheek, and she knew this would be a memory she would have for the rest of her life. Too bad for Bethany, it wasn't going to be a pleasant one. We wanted you to keep thinking you were on top because it was going to be so sweet when you realized you would never be more than a pathetic wannabe stuck in the gallows.

****

"Doing something romantic for Emily?" Elizabeth asked, sitting down watching Tucker make a bonfire.

Tucker turned to Elizabeth. "Why can't you just leave me alone?"

She chuckled. "Why should I? You ruined my life with what you did."

"But it was an accident."

She stood up. "Was it? Did you plan on hitting me with your car that night? It seemed you wanted something for your new project. Who knows what's lurking in your dark, twisted mind?"

"It was an accident. You've left me alone all this time. Why can't you continue to do it?"

"Because you forgot about me. You were starting to live a happy life."

"I was happy with Bethany."

Elizabeth rolled her eyes. "Please, we all knew you weren't happy with her. You were bottling up all your emotions. You kept me repressed for so long."

Tucker took a seat. "So, if I hadn't started talking to Emily about you, then I wouldn't be haunted by you?"

Elizabeth laughed. "Isn't that a bitch?"

Emily walked up right then. "Tucker, did you go to all this trouble?" she asked.

Tucker turned to her and smiled. "Yeah, I thought we could have a romantic night since tomorrow is my last day of school."

Emily smiled because she needed this. It felt good to be with someone that didn't have pain or demons attacking him. Emily, you should have waited a couple more minutes before making those assumptions. He had demons, and he was about to let it be known.

He got up and kissed her on the lips. He embraced the kiss, and he was hoping by focusing on the kiss, he would lose Elizabeth in the process. "That's so sweet; the murderer knows how to kiss. Hope this isn't her last one knowing you."

"Leave me the fuck alone!" Tucker snapped.

Emily looked at him confused. "Is everything all right?" she asked.

He looked around. He couldn't see Elizabeth anymore. He thought maybe she would give him peace. "Yeah, I just had a moment."

Emily looked at him and touched his arm. "Is there something you aren't telling me?" she asked.

"Yeah, Tucker. Do you want to tell her what really happened that night?" Elizabeth asked.

Tucker ignored Elizabeth. "I guess, I'm stressed out about tomorrow being my last day of high school. I never thought it would actually happen, but here we are."

Emily grabbed his hand. "It's okay to be scared."

"You don't know what he's going through. He hasn't even told you how he took pictures of me as I was dying. My last image of the world was my killer putting a camera lens in my face," Elizabeth whispered into Tucker's ear.

Tucker, we had no clue you were such a sick fuck. Maybe Elizabeth was right about you. Did you really want her dead? What kind of normal human being would take photos of a person before calling the cops? She could have lived.

"Fuck you!" he screamed, and pushed Emily thinking that it was Elizabeth.

Emily fell to the ground. She saw a side of Tucker that she wasn't enjoying. "What is going on with you?" She knew he was having an episode.

He ran his fingers through his hair. "I didn't plan to take those photos. It came to my mind. I knew after I took them that it was wrong. I should have called 911 first. I know that."

"But you kept the photos," Elizabeth said.

"I didn't mean to. I just thought it could be used against me."

Emily stood up. "What are you talking about?" she asked.

Tucker looked at Emily. He saw all the worry on her face. "You caused this," he said. He remembered what Elizabeth said.

"What?"

Tucker grabbed Emily by her shirt. "You caused her to come back. I didn't want to talk about her, but you forced it out of me." He let go of Emily and leaned back. "You made me do this."

"Who?" Emily was confused where all of this was coming from. She was trying to play along, but Tucker was all over the place.

"Elizabeth. I didn't want to talk about the accident, but you made me."

This was what got Emily upset. "You came to me. I wasn't planning to ever speak to you after what you did to Andrew."

"Andrew." It clicked in Tucker's mind. "You cause these good people to ruin their lives." He stood up. "You did that to me, Andrew, and Matthew."

Emily slapped him across the face. "I didn't do any of it. You three caused me to be the person I am. I'm broken because I tried to help you assholes out, and I'm getting the blame because you three weren't strong enough." She grabbed her bag. "I didn't do anything wrong," she turned and walked away.

Tucker let her go because he didn't know what else to say. He was trying to get his emotions in check right now, and he knew she was right to some degree. He hadn't been strong enough, because Elizabeth wouldn't be back in his life if he were.

Emily stormed toward the elevator. She got in and fell to her knees crying. She thought Tucker was different. She thought she was over all this drama. She pulled out her phone, and she called the one person she wanted to forget.

He answered quickly. "I never thought I would hear from you again,"

Emily hated his voice, but she needed him in this moment. "I need to pick up."

"For you, anything. See you soon." He hung up before she could respond.

She got up and fixed herself. She would escape these demons, and she would forget about Tucker, Andrew, and Matthew.

Tucker stood there looking at the door Emily walked out of. Tucker heard Elizabeth clapping. "Bravo."

He turned to her. "Fuck you. I'm done with your bullshit. I'm getting rid of you right now." He got up and walked toward his room. He grabbed the folder that he buried in one of his desk drawers. He didn't even need to look at the photos. They were a series of photos of Elizabeth dying on the ground. In each of the photos, you could see her life slowly leave her eyes. He even took a photo of her last breath and after.

He tossed them in the fire. "Now, I can be done with you." Tucker believed this was his chance to forget all about what he did to Elizabeth. He was about to graduate high school, and he wanted all of this to stay in the past.

Tucker, you should learn by now that nothing stays in the past. We really hoped you would get some strength, because we had a feeling Elizabeth wasn't going away anytime soon. You would also have to deal with the blood on your hands from Emily. You had better be worried about the call she just made. This couple was a train wreck, and we couldn't wait for the destruction.

Chapter 37

"Can you believe it's our last day of high school?" Aman asked, walking up to Calvin.

Calvin turned to Aman and smiled. They hadn't really talked since their hook up session in the dugout. They both nodded when it was over and walked their separate ways. Both of them didn't want to admit that they thought of it for the past couple of nights.

Calvin looked around at the kids cheering as they were cleaning out their lockers. Danielle had ditched early because she had a client to see. "I thought this day would never come, but I feel it came too fast."

Aman nodded. "It's going to be weird never walking through these halls ever again."

"We still have graduation rehearsal and cap and gown fittings." Calvin paused. "But I know what you mean. We've all been dying to get out of these halls, and now it's here."

"Do you regret what happened the other day?" Aman asked. He had been worried that it would send Calvin into a tailspin. Aman, you had to already know he was in rock bottom. You just added salt to the wound.

Calvin shook his head. "No, I don't. It was nice to reconnect." Calvin saw Coach Soto look at him. "I better go. I'll see you around."

Aman wanted to tell Calvin something, but he couldn't find the courage. "Yeah, we will talk later." Aman saw Calvin walk over to Coach Soto. He walked to his locker and grabbed the remainder of his things. He saw Delilah at her locker looking over papers, and he didn't know where Danielle was. They were the popular kids until prom, and now they were nothing more than alumni of this school.

"I can't believe you're graduating," Coach Soto said, when Calvin walked up to him.

Calvin played with the strap on his bag. "I wished it ended on better terms, but here we are."

"You've always been a fighter." Coach Soto had to ask Calvin something. He was worried about him lately. "I saw you and Aman in the dugout the other day when I was cleaning out the supply shed."

Calvin blushed and looked away. "Yeah, that was a moment of weakness."

"Have you been having a lot of those lately?" Coach Soto asked.

Yes Calvin, why didn't you tell him all about your late-night affairs? Should you tell him how you have an appointment with a clinic after this? "I've been trying to figure myself out lately. That's not a crime, right?"

"No, but you shouldn't be exposing yourself or losing yourself in something."

"I don't know what I am now. Coach, I was the popular baseball player."

"Now, you're a graduate, and you like boys. There's nothing wrong with a new identifier." You were right, Coach. The only problem was he didn't like this identifier.

Calvin looked down at his shoes. "I just want to have a purpose again, or something that excitements me."

Coach Soto placed a hand on Calvin's shoulder. "You'll find something. You just need to be patient and believe that it's going to all work out."

Calvin felt his phone go off. It was a reminder that he had an appointment. "I better get going. I have somewhere I need to be."

"No problem. I want you to look back on these hallways with fond memories. I want you to be able to walk in these halls in ten years and be proud of the legacy you are about to create."

"Thanks, Coach." Calvin walked out the halls for the last time as a student of Johnson Prep. He took Coach Soto's words to heart, but he knew that he wouldn't leave a legacy he would be proud of. He didn't think a kid his age had to go to the clinic because he might have caught something. Here was to hoping you came back positive, we mean negative.

****

"We will have quick results back in a couple of days. If we find something, we will contact you for further testing," the nurse said with a smile.

Calvin smiled. "Thank you, I guess."

"It's nothing you should be worried about. People have scares all the times. Maybe for the future, you should use condoms and not have so many different partners." The nurse looked at the clipboard. "I'll be back with your papers, and you'll be set to go."

Calvin moaned and laid back. "Aman, why did you have to stay in the closet?" he asked out loud. He knew if Aman came out, that none of this would be happening. Calvin closed his eyes.

Calvin felt his phone go off. He pulled it out to see a text from a mysterious number.

Unknown: *Calvin, you were such prize eye candy for all the girls and boys of Johnson Prep. You had everything going for you; popularity, baseball, and you could have had anyone in the school. It looks like your declaration at prom made you go downhill. Maybe next time you decide to be everyone's thirst trap you should be more careful. We wouldn't want the school to find out your new favorite extracurricular activity was going to the free clinic. Give us dirt on your best friend Danielle, and we can forget this whole thing happened. -The Revenged Queen."*

Calvin's heart dropped. The last thing he wanted was for this to get out to the whole school. The other problem was he wasn't going to expose Danielle like that. He wouldn't betray her because she has never betrayed him. Calvin, you had better think fast, because The Revenged Queen had you by your cock, and she wasn't stroking it. Hoped you enjoyed blue balls on your status at Johnson Prep. Graduation was the finish line of your years at the school, but it could also be the death of your reputation.

Chapter 38

It was truly a tragic moment to see the current reigning queen alone in her castle for her own party. Bethany thought people were showing up late, but people had other plans. They were all at Jordan's end of the year party. Bethany was trying to make memories, and we had to admit that this was moment we wouldn't forget.

Bethany was chugging a bottle of champagne when she heard the door open. "Hello?" Jordan shouted out.

Bethany walked from the living room to the foyer to see Jordan standing there with a smug look on her face. She crossed her arms. "Came to gloat that everyone's at your party?" Bethany said, trying to compose herself.

Jordan laughed for a moment. "It's quite enjoyable to see your rise to the top was ended so quickly." Jordan handed her flowers. "It's custom during a funeral to give flowers."

Bethany took the flowers. "No one's dead."

"Your reputation is." Jordan walked past her into the living. "So, this is where The Marked Queen lives. It's a wholesome home." She turned to look at Bethany. "I can see where the wallflower in you came out."

"I don't need this. Won't people realize that you're missing?" Bethany asked.

Jordan didn't turn around. "No one ever knows where the host of a party is. They assume she's mingling, drinking, or in my case, fucking a whole football team."

"I don't regret posting about you," Bethany said. "I don't regret anything that I did." Bethany was proud of everything she had accomplished as The Marked Queen. She was more upset that it didn't translate after everything went down.

"And I don't think anyone should regret how ruthless you've been." Jordan turned around. "How you have ruined lives, friendships, and status at Johnson Prep?"

"I wanted to make a name for myself."

Jordan could respect her for that. She was trying to be more than the party girl. She wanted to be the ruthless bitch now. "Well you succeeded."

Bethany chuckled. "Really? I'm still the wallflower everyone forgets about." She played with her hair. "I even got a stupid makeover thinking it would change things." Bethany felt like a complete failure. She wanted to believe that she got things right. She was disappointed that nothing worked out for her. Bethany, you were adored by the mystery of yourself. You should have never come out of the closet. You should have learned that tale from Calvin.

"People hate you for exposing all their truths."

"And you don't think the rejects of the school don't hate you for ruining our lives?"

Jordan shrugged. "I assumed it was because of your jealousy for us."

"And that's why I created The Marked Queen. Your smugness is what caused your downfall." That was rich coming from you, Bethany. We thought the same about your demise.

"You really feel like you did good with her?" Jordan had a flashback to Shane on top of her. "You didn't think that the repercussion from your little Marked Days wasn't going to ruin people?"

"You all deserved it."

"Clara had to move. She was so close to graduating, but she left because her pregnancy got out. She hadn't even told her parents."

"She was the same bitch that came into the bathroom after I bled all over my dress, because of my stupid period. Instead of being a good person, she took pictures and told the whole school." Bethany paused. "I don't care if she was sent off, because she deserved it."

"So, it's okay to get revenge on someone that humiliates you?" Jordan asked.

"If they deserve it, then yes."

"And you're not worried about The Revenged Queen?" Jordan asked another question. She was curious how she would respond to this question.

Bethany had now heard of The Revenged Queen, but there wasn't anything to worry about. She took care of her scandal, and she was paying the other guy to keep her other secret safe. She knew there was nothing about her that this new queen would find out. She also assumed it was some sophomore trying to take over now that the seniors were done.

"Why would I be scared when I'm out of high school?"

Jordan nodded her head. "I think you're being naïve. We all thought we were invincible until you came around."

"That was the point of her." Bethany looked around. "I wanted you people to feel how I did for so many years."

"And I hope someone gets you back, because you've caused a lot of pain in people's lives, too."

"Jordan, you're one of the most popular girls in this school. You could have anyone you truly wanted. I've done nothing to ruin your life."

Jordan wanted to tell her right then. She wanted to expose to Bethany how much she had ruined her life. Jordan just smiled and put on the mask. "You're right. I'm just being a dramatic bitch, I guess." She felt her phone go off. It was a text from Alassane asking where she was. She smiled because finally someone noticed she was gone. She had been doing it for years to see if people really even noticed if she was there.

"I better get back to my party. I have so many peasants to please. Enjoy your self-pity. It was quite an enjoyable sight. Maybe this will prove to you that you can never climb the social ladder, it's all bullshit." She turned and left Bethany to her sad, lonely thoughts.

Bethany wanted to believe that she would have one memory with friends and laughter. Bethany, you created your final memories: sadness, backstabbing, and scandal. Of course, you weren't going to have any generic memories. You should be proud of what you accomplished and stop being a whiney bitch about it, because you would truly have something to be depressed about in only a few short days.

****

It was rather enjoyable to see our favorite fallen queen slumming it in a stranger's bed in a random hotel. Danielle, we thought you had higher morals than that. We guess we were wrong. You really did want to enjoy your last day as a Johnson Prep student in style.

Danielle opened her eyes, and she had no clue where she was. She turned to see a strange man in her bed, and she didn't even know where she was or how she got there. She quietly got out of bed and grabbed her clothes. She looked around at the hotel room, and it was completely trashed . There were empty alcohol bottles, cocaine, and clothes scattered around.

Danielle tried to remember one thing from last night. She was supposed to meet up with Christian and a client, and they were supposed to have a three way. She remembered not being into it, but she doesn't remember anything else. She looked around for her phone, and she found it on the floor near the bathroom.

She walked into the bathroom and closed the door. She quickly called Christian. He picked up on the second ring. "How's my movie star doing?"

"Where the fuck are you?"

"I thought you and Owen wanted to have some private time. He paid for the whole night with you."

"Are you now my pimp?" she asked in anger.

He laughed. "Haven't I been this whole time?" He paused. "Why do you sound so angry?"

"I thought we were doing this as partners. You left me in a strange hotel room, and I don't know what happened last night."

Christian sighed. "I figured it was self-explained. We met up with Owen to have our three-way. Well, you were going to have sex with him, I was just watching. He wanted you, but I knew you would say no if I wasn't involved."

"Damn right."

"And I gave you something to take the edge off. You were quite the show last night," Christian said.

It took a minute for Danielle to process what he just said to her. "Did you fucking drug me?"

"If you need to put a label on things."

Danielle had never felt more ashamed or used in her life. She thought she had power here when it came to her new job, but she was starting to realize she was right back in someone's hands getting home. "I'll go to the police."

He laughed. "And tell them what?" He sent Danielle the video of her from last night. "No cop is going to believe you were going against your will."

Danielle clicked on the video Christian sent her. It was all three of them in the hotel room. Danielle was all over both of them. She was kissing on Owen and trying to give Christian a hand job. She stopped once Christian's dick came out. Danielle, why would you stop the video? We wanted to see how well he used that amazing package of his. You shouldn't feel ashamed, because we would all trade places with you, well, minus the drugging part.

"I can't believe you would do this to me. I'll tell someone," she said. "You're not going to get away with this."

"And then we both go down. Danielle, the moment you tell people about me drugging you, then my site goes down. I'll post this video everywhere, and you won't make it out alive."

"So, you're blackmailing me?" she asked.

"Exactly."

"I fucking hate you."

"You're just mad you enjoyed it too much last night." He laughed and hung up on her. He grabbed his glass of champagne, and he continued to watch the video of Danielle going down on him. He felt himself getting hard. He looked up to see his own client walking in. She was a beautiful blonde, and he was ready to have his way with her. This fetish site was really picking up and one of the people who caused that, wasn't willing to celebrate at the moment.

Danielle wanted to fall apart right then, but she couldn't. She wanted to be safe in her home where she didn't need to think about any of this. She left the bathroom and grabbed the rest of her things. She closed her eyes and tried to stop the flashbacks of Christian forcing her to drink something as she rode in her taxi home.

She walked into her house to see her mom standing there. "Late night on the streets?"

"Mom, I'm not in the mood." She really didn't need her mother harping on her right now. She was about to have a mental breakdown, and she just wanted to do it in privacy.

Lily didn't say anything else. She looked her daughter up and down. "Wash your face. I know you're a cheap whore, but you don't need to look like one." Lily opened the door to the house and walked out.

Danielle walked into the bathroom and locked the door. She crawled into the shower and let the water cool her emotions. She closed her eyes. She started to remember some things from last night. "I don't feel so good," she said.

"You're finally loosening up," Christian said.

Danielle tried to push away. "Let me go."

Christian turned on the camera. "Do you want to disappoint all your fans? People finally love you again, Danielle. Do you want to lose them?"

Danielle shook her head. She didn't want to be a reject again. "No, I don't."

Christian started to unzip his pants. "Let's give them a show."

Danielle opened her eyes, and she felt the tears falling down her face. She knew that she had made a complete mess of things, and she didn't know how she was going to fix them. She was supposed to be celebrating getting out the toxic ways of Johnson Prep. Danielle, you were leaving quite the legacy for other kids to remember you by. You had better get used to crying because this secret would soon be exposed.

Chapter 39

Emily sat there, and she didn't know how else to feel. She closed her eyes praying the breeze would calm her nerves. She knew she could cry here. Many people had. She was surrounded by death, and in this moment, she felt the most at peace.

She looked at a text from Tucker. He had apologized for his outburst, but she knew that he was telling the truth. "I did cause him to have his meltdown. I was the one that made him talk about his emotions. He was trying to figure out how to run away from the stigma from the car accident." She shook her head. "He wasn't trying to look for therapy."

She pulled out a letter from Andrew. He also attached a photo of him in the woods. He had only been gone for a couple of weeks, but he seemed like he was getting centered. She read the note out loud since there was no one here that was going to argue with her.

Dear Emily,

I have spent the last couple of weeks trying to regroup as a human being. I've tried to find peace with my mother's death. I have found comfort in knowing that I'm not like every other kid. I've dealt with tragedy, and I've had to overcome them. I'm an alcoholic, and I can't shy away from that. I've also spent the time trying to process all the people that I've hurt. You were the biggest person I've betrayed. You were my source of escape, and you didn't deserve that. You didn't deserve the hurtful things that I've said or when I hit you. I plan to come home in the next couple of weeks. I would love to see you and work on our relationship.

Love, Andrew

That was such a sweet letter, Andrew. We were disappointed that you finally got your shit together, but there always needed to be a happy ending, right? Emily just laughed out loud. "Did you hear that? He wants to fix everything between us." She crumbled up the piece of paper. "He doesn't get it that I don't want things to work out between us. There's only one person I really want to be with," she said.

Emily was sitting at a bench at Mathew Ryan's grave. She clung to his letterman jacket with such disdained. "Do you hear that, Matt? I have guys wanting to be with me." She threw the letter at his gravesite. "Why couldn't that be from you?" She asked.

"Because I couldn't handle my demons," Matthew said sitting on the bench. He wasn't in his normal football gear that he caught her eye in. He was in converse, black pants, and a plaid shirt. It was what he normally wore for their dates. His curly hair was covered by a beanie, and she still melted into his hazel eyes. She looked at his dark skin and was always envious of how smooth it was.

"Right? I'm the girl that attracts all the guys who can't get their shit together."

Matthew stood up. "I don't want you to hate yourself for what we did. We thought we could be strong for you. We wanted to be your foundation."

"I didn't need any of you to be my foundation!" she screamed at him. She knew if someone saw her, they would think she was crazy. "I needed someone to love me."

Matthew tried to grab her hand. "I love you."

She stepped back from him. "No, you didn't. You wouldn't have done what you did."

"Ems. I was scared, okay?"

"But what about me? Why did you have to leave me? I'm stuck without your stupid smile, your cocky attitude when you beat me at fucking video games, and the way you would lead when we danced under the stars." Emily felt the tears fall down her face.

He laughed. "We did make a beautiful pair when we danced, and it wasn't my fault that you sucked at Smash."

His comment caused there to be less tension in the air. She shook her head, and she had a smile on her face. "This is why I fell for you."

His smile faltered. "You need to move on. I'm gone, but you aren't. I'll always love you, but we wouldn't have worked out in the end. I was a dangerous guy that took an innocent girl and ruined her life."

Emily looked Matthew in the eyes. "Matt, I hate you for framing me as your murderer. I hate you for making me turn into this girl that tries to heal broken men." She paused. "But I love you for making me that stupid girl in your letterman jacket. I love you for making me that stupid girl you danced with under the stars. I hate you for deciding to let me find you that way, but I love you for making me believe I was special."

She closed her eyes and opened them again. He wasn't there anymore. She took a seat on the bench. "But I'll bring you back," she said. She pulled out a needle, and a rubber band. She tied it around her arm. She tapped her arm a couple of times to find the vein. She took in a deep breath. "You were an idiot to think I was some innocent girl." She injected herself with the heroin. She ignored the pain, because it was worth losing herself in the numbness. She closed her eyes counting the seconds until the pain in her heart would go away.

Tucker, Andrew, and Matthew, what have you done? Emily was no longer the girl people got wrong. She no longer had been misidentified. She had opened her hearts to you, but she kept getting beaten up by your demons. She couldn't do it anymore, and we wondered what would happen to her. Emily felt herself slowly losing consciousness, but the one memory she had was the moonlight dancing off Matthew's face.

****

"What do you mean I'm tied?" Bethany asked. She had been called into the guidance office before graduation rehearsal. She had assumed it was to go over her speech, which she had finished months ago.

"We went over everyone's GPA's. You and Hilary Bloom were tied for the best GPA," Ms. Diop said.

"You also said that I was failing my classes, and you were wrong about that." Bethany stood up.

Ms. Diop stood up also. "Yes, we were wrong about your poor grades after looking over the books again, but we feel certain about this."

Bethany rolled her eyes. "I doubt it." She turned and stormed out of the room. She went straight for the computer lab. She wasn't surprised to see Carter to still be in there. "You do know that yesterday was our last day as students, right?"

Carter looked up to see Bethany standing there. He shouldn't be surprised to see her. He was waiting for this interaction. "I'm just killing time before we have graduation rehearsal." He didn't even know why he had to be here for this stupid thing. He wasn't giving a speech, and no one would care if he missed it. He was pissed his sister and mother guilted him into going today.

Bethany put her purse down. "Bullshit. You're hacking something, and it had better be the school records again."

"Why? You're on top."

"I'm fucking tied for valedictorian." Bethany looked around. They had the room to themselves. We didn't know why she waited until now to see if someone was in there, but clearly she lost her smarts. "I'm fucking tied with Hilary Bloom." Bethany crossed her arms. "That Asian bitch will not be the fucking valedictorian."

"Why? She earned it." Carter asked. He liked messing with her, and he found some enjoyment out of it.

Bethany slammed her hand on the desk. "I earned that spot, and you know damn well I did. You had better fucking fix this."

Carter crossed his arms. "Or what? It looks like I have all the power here."

Bethany laughed. "Really?" She pulled out her phone and place it in front of him. "Isn't this your ad for helping out the students of Johnson Prep."

He grabbed the phone. "Everyone was supposed to get rid of that when I accepted the job."

"You really trust people that way. How cute is that?" Bethany knew she had the upper hand. What she didn't know was that Carter wanted her to keep this ad. He wanted to see if she had truly changed. He encoded the email ad with a virus, so he had access to everyone's computer. He knew when to destroy the evidence if he needed to.

"I like to believe that people have good intentions."

"I guess I don't. I want what I paid you for, you piece of shit."

Zachary Ryan

"You really are The Marked Queen. What happened to just trying to ruin the social order? What happened to the girl just wanting to get revenge for what they did to you?"

"Well, I got distracted with that bullshit, and I want what I came for. You had better give it to me, or I'll be The Marked Queen again." She paused. "You don't want your obese girlfriend to find out, do you?"

Carter looked at her. "You're such a bitch, and yet, you act like you have a heart."

She shrugged. "I have a heart when I need to. I have worked too damn hard for this. I will be standing in front of you pathetic losers giving a speech that will move you all to damn tears." She looked him right in the face.

He stood up. "You're still the cruel bitch looking for worshippers. They're going to eventually realize that you're all bullshit."

She picked up her purse. "People are going to remember my name forever in these halls. I doubt we can say that about you."

"I don't want to be out the shadows," Carter said. He didn't see the appeal of being in the spotlight. Bethany, he could have been Mr. Popular. He was hot, athletic, smart, and he could have had any girl in the school. He chose to be with Jasmine for whatever pathetic reason, but it kept him off people's radars.

"Everyone wants to be in the spotlight." She grabbed her phone. "You better fix this, or you won't have anywhere to hide." She turned and walked out of the room.

Carter was disappointed with Bethany's actions, but he knew he shouldn't have been surprised. He had a backup plan, and he was going to give Bethany exactly what she wanted. He called Jordan. "I have more dirt on Bethany if you want it." He hung up on Jordan after she agreed to get the information out of him.

Bethany, you should have realized that you created a game of blackmail. You made people use their enemies' skeletons against them. It was going to be so tragic when they used yours against you. You had better get your speech ready, but you were the only one going to be moved to tears once The Revenged Queen was done with you.

****

"I got this after I went to the doctors to get tested," Calvin said. He handed over his phone to Danielle. They were standing in entrance of the building they plan to graduate from. He wanted to talk to her about the text before they went into graduation rehearsal. He knew he could never betray Danielle the way The Revenged Queen wanted, but he didn't want it to get out that he might have an STI.

Danielle didn't look at the text yet. She was more worried about Calvin. "Is everything okay?" she asked.

He shrugged. He wanted to tell her the truth that his life was completely a mess, but he didn't want to get into it right before they had to sit during a boring rehearsal. "I'm fine. I just wanted to double check that I didn't have anything. I wouldn't worry about it too much."

Danielle looked at him, but she ignored it. She knew that he would tell her if something was going to go wrong. Yes Danielle, since you both were telling each other everything going on. Did he know about you waking up alone in a hotel room? Calvin, we wondered if you told her about you and Aman hooking up?

She read the text, and she felt anger in her bones. She knew the moment she finished the text who it came from. "That fucking bitch."

"I know. I can't believe this Revenged Queen wants me to rat you out."

Danielle rolled her eyes. "You know damn well it's Delilah."

"What?"

"She's still fucking not over that I gave her secrets to Bethany over yours." Danielle thought they were over this bullshit. She was stupid to think that their conversation that night would fix anything. Danielle, you were played, but we wondered what you were going to do about it.

"So... what do we do?" Calvin asked. He knew that Danielle would fix it. She wasn't the type of girl to let anything go.

"Don't you worry, Calvin. I'm about to show this bitch what she can do with her fucking threats," Danielle said. She turned and walked away from Calvin.

Danielle burst open the doors to the banquet room they planned to have their graduation ceremony in. People were sitting in their seats listening to the instructor. Delilah was standing in the front with Bethany and another student. Bethany received a message that she would be giving the speech.

"You fucking bitch!" Danielle screamed. The room went silent, and people looked at Danielle. They had no clue what was going on, but you kids were in for good bitch fight.

Danielle stormed the aisle until she was right in front of Delilah. "You really couldn't let it go, you fucking cockroach." She slapped Delilah across the face. They said that people at

Johnson Prep didn't get violent, but they had to change that saying now.

Delilah felt the pain go across her face. Delilah felt the rage fill her body. She had enough of Danielle. Delilah lunged forward at Danielle, but she wasn't expecting Delilah to fight back. They both fell to the ground. People started getting their phones out and recording the cat fight.

There were screams, hair pulling, scratches, and a story that made this boring rehearsal way more interesting. We were disappointed that Calvin and Mr. Rozengota had to break them up.

Danielle and Delilah fixed themselves up. Mr. Rozengota grabbed both of their hands and pulled them to a side room. "You two will stay in here and fix whatever issues you're having. If you don't come out of here in a civil manner, neither one of you may attend the graduation ceremony." Mr. Rozengota slammed the door and walked away.

"You really can't let go what I did," Danielle said.

"You were my best friend, and I was at my lowest. I thought you would never betray me like that."

"Whatever happened to letting it all go after we talked?"

Delilah crossed her arms. "I was acting."

"Clearly." Danielle looked at Delilah. She was over it. "You know what? Post whatever bullshit you want. It's not going to change anything. I don't know who you're working with, but they will be your only friends."

"Who says I didn't do this on my own?"

"Coming from the bitch that was getting rammed by the principal to get her grades up and cutting herself because she had low self-esteem, I doubt you have the smarts or balls to be The Revenged Queen all by yourself." Danielle had a point. You were so much better as a sidekick, but you did know how to defend yourself in a cat fight.

"You deserve everything coming your way. You backstabbed friends to get ahead."

Danielle shook her head. "And you're even worse than The Marked Queen. You complain and whine like some sad spoiled girl about how I hurt you. I don't regret exposing you, because I know damn well Calvin is loyal to me and a true friend. You want to say The Marked Queen was this horrid bitch, but you're doing exactly what she did. This is why you were always an annoying sidekick and never a queen. You're as fragile as the male ego."

Delilah looked Danielle right in the eyes. "But I have all the power. I can expose your ass right now. Your whole life would be ruined."

Danielle shrugged. She was done with all of this bullshit. She was tired of popularity. It had bitten her in the ass way too many times. She thought being adored by her school would make her feel rich, and instead, she turned into a prostitute. What would you turn to now that you realized you didn't like being a wet dream fantasy anymore? You thought you were about to be out of that world, but you caused a lot of men to be very satisfied.

"Expose me, bitch. See if I give a damn." She went for the door. "At least I'll have a friend to go to when the chips are down."

"And you were supposed to be mine, but you were the one that pushed the chips," Delilah said.

Danielle opened the door. "Once again. It's all part of the game. No one likes a weak villain, so pick. Villain or victim, not both." Danielle walked out the room. She saw Mr. Rozengota standing there. "Don't worry Mr. Rozengota, Delilah and I are best friends again. She's coming over later, so we can braid each other's hair and play with each other's vaginas." Danielle didn't give him a chance to respond before she walked towards the entrance of the building.

Delilah, that was how to be a bad ass queen. You were lurking behind your little phone and praying someone would betray a close friend. You had better learn from Danielle because she might have had her moments of regret, but she didn't cry over them. Well, she might once she realized how her skeletons had a chain around her neck. The question still remained for you Delilah, did you want to cry about a friend betraying you, or did you want to get revenge on the bitch?

Chapter 40

"Why didn't you give me this sooner?" Jordan asked, once Carter told her about the abortion. Carter had given her the medical files for the abortion and her actual grades she had before he changed them for her.

"I thought she was different. I understood what it meant to try to take down the popular group. You guys believe you're better than everyone, and you live a life of recklessness. I don't think you truly understand how mortal you are." Carter wanted to believe that Bethany only was a bitch to prove to the world how horrible the royal court of Johnson Prep was, but she had turned The Marked Queen monster into a realty.

Jordan looked at the information Carter gave to her. "I think she did a great job of showing us all that we aren't untouchable." She paused for a moment. "But it doesn't change the fact that she opened Pandora's box. She deserves this."

"That's why I'm giving it to you. She's become the same evil person she tried to stop," Carter said. He held so much anger in his heart toward Bethany for exposing Jasmine the way she did. He hoped Jordan followed through.

Jordan touched his arm. "You don't need to defend Jasmine's honor anymore." She grabbed her things. "Tomorrow is going to be one hell of a day." She kissed Carter on the cheek. "Thanks so much."

Jordan walked out of the lab seeing Alassane walking up to her. "What are you doing here?" he asked.

She quickly put the files in her purse. "I was finishing up a homework assignment. I'm not as lucky as you and get to ignore the rest of the school year." She wanted to deflect the conversation onto him. "What are you doing here?" she asked.

He lifted up his cap and gown. "I had to grab my cap and gown. I didn't know why they couldn't have it at the rehearsal place, but at least I got to see you."

Jordan rolled her eyes. "Are you trying to be corny?"

He laughed. "I think it's working. You missed quite the cat fight between Danielle and Delilah."

"Don't worry, I saw the video." The video between Danielle and Delilah quickly went viral thanks to Aman posting it on his channel. The two girls promised they kissed and made up, but we had a feeling they were lying.

Alassane was happy to run into Jordan. "I wanted to talk to you about the other night."

Jordan waved him off. "We don't need to talk about it. I was drunk, and I was depressed."

Alassane went to grab her hand. "Are you sure? You know I'm a friend."

She pulled her hand away before he could grab it. "I'm fine. You don't need to look at me like I'm some fragile girl."

"That's not what I meant. I just wanted to tell you that you aren't alone."

Jordan saw a couple of guys coming this way. "I better get going. I hope to see you tomorrow."

Alassane wanted to say more, but he didn't want to force her into talking to him. He lifted his cap and gown. "I'll be the one wearing red."

Jordan walked away. Eddie and a couple of guys walked up to Alassane. "Was that Jordan Caraway?" Eddie asked.

"Yeah, she's a friend of mine."

Eddie laughed. "No one is friends with Jordan." Oh Eddie, you were still the dumbest quarterback on the football team. Thank god you can throw a ball around, because no other college or girl is going to fall in love with you.

"She's actually a great person."

Eddie shrugged. "She's a slut. She banged half the athletes in this school. It's probably why she was talking to you," Eddie said, and it caused his friends to laugh.

Jordan heard the whole thing. She swallowed up her pride and kept walking. She knew Alassane was defending her, and she thought that was sweet. Eddie's comments ignited a fire under her ass. She has spent the last couple of days lost in her feelings, and she wasn't going to let her self-doubts ruin her mission.

She had everything she needed for her graduation reveal, and we were ready for it. She pulled out her phone, and she wanted all the graduates to have something to savor before she came wrecking all their phone.

Jordan: *Congrats to the class of 2018. You all were about to say your goodbyes to this school for the very last time. There will be tears, heartbreak, and overall sadness, and I'm not talking about the ceremony. This class has caused a lot of damage over the years, and I thought it was time for the truth to come out. Hope you were a model student all four years to your classmates, because tomorrow might be a rough ending for you. You all can wear your hideous red gowns, but you'll be remembering the bitch in the black dress that delivered karma's message. Sleep tight tonight, boys and girls, because tomorrow is going to be one hell of a storm. -The Revenged Queen. Jordan hit send and was ready to prove to the school she wasn't just a bargain harlot.*

Chapter 41

Tucker opened the door to see Emily standing there. He had spent the last hour taking photos with his parents before they left for the graduation ceremony. "You came?"

Emily had a smile on her face. "I told you that I would come."

"I know, but I thought that you wouldn't after how I treated you."

Emily moved forward and kissed Tucker on the lips. She had spent the last day getting high off her ass. She danced with Matthew to their favorite songs, she looked at the stars with him, and she got to be with the person she loved. The high ran off, and she needed someone to help her with the crash.

"We all have our moments, and we say things are aren't fully proud of." She paused. "I can't believe you're graduating today."

Tucker looked down at his ugly red gown. Why was it that no graduation gown looked good on anyone? Couldn't someone make a sexier one? We would ask Danielle, but she was too busy sucking cock for money, well according to a video that could come out.

"I never thought this day would come." He paused, trying to ignore thinking about the car accident. "Do you want anything to drink?" He asked.

"I just want to freshen up before we go, do you mind if I use the bathroom?" she asked.

He shook his head. His parents were probably in their room watching baby videos. They had been doing that all day crying because he was growing up. "The third door on the left. I'm going to go upstairs real quick to grab my camera bag."

He went upstairs to see Elizabeth sitting on the bed. "Did you really think you could get rid of me that easily?"

"What do you want from me? I got rid of the photos. I know I'm sorry. What more do you want?"

Elizabeth stood up. "I want my life back."

"I can't give that to you." Tucker looked away from her. "I would give it to you if I could. I don't deserve to be here. You were a mother and a wife. You were doing good in this world, and I killed you."

"Isn't that a cruel irony? The evil lives on, and the good die young."

Tucker looked at her. "Please, I need you to give me some kind of peace. I need to know how I'm able to get rid of you."

She laughed. "That's the problem with you. You only want to get rid of me, but you don't want to cleanse your soul. I'll be here for a very long time. You should have thought about that when you decided to do what you did. I'm not going anywhere anytime soon. Have fun going crazy and ruining your life. You shouldn't have one after you took mine," Elizabeth said. She walked out of the room leaving Tucker feeling defeated.

Tucker's Mom, Terry walked into the room. She was on the heavier side with dirty blonde hair, cheap manicure, and she wore glasses that were always a slight askew on her. It didn't make sense she didn't wear glasses that fit. Bitch, you had money. You should be acting like it.

"Honey, what's wrong?" she asked, taking a seat next to her son.

Yes Tucker, why didn't you tell your mother the real reason you were down? I bet she would completely understand. It wouldn't make you look crazy or anything. "I just have a lot of emotions going through me right now. I never thought this day would come after everything that happened."

Terry pulled Tucker close. "Tuck, it was an accident. I know you'll live with that guilt for the rest of your life, but you need to remember that you're a good person, and you'll be fine." Terry, you were so blinded by your love for your son...and maybe waffles. He didn't tell you the full truth, and we were dying for your reaction once it happened.

"Thanks, mom." It didn't make Tucker feel better, but it was a start. "I need to go check on Emily."

Terry's face lit up. "Emily came? I can't wait to meet her."

"Yeah, she's downstairs right now." Tucker was pleased to know at least one thing was going well in his life. He should have stayed a wallflower, then he wouldn't have come off this stupid.

What they didn't know was what Emily was doing in the guest bathroom. She was currently pulling out her needles, her favorite rubber band, and her favorite way of passing the time. Yes, Emily came back to you, but she only did by body. You better hope this addiction was a fleeting one, because we were about to have another Matthew Ryan on our hands. We wondered who would be walking in on her crime scene. We hoped it was Tucker, because he was already an expert on photo series of people's final breaths.

****

Delilah sat down in her cap and gown waiting for her mother to take her to graduation. She was holding a photo of her and her dad when she was little. She wanted nothing more than for her father to be here as she said her goodbyes to

Johnson Prep. She sighed, knowing it would never happen. Delilah, you shouldn't be so glum. If you wanted someone to be there that you could call daddy, why not give Richard a ring? We knew how much you loved to be so close to him. He has been terribly upset you haven't returned his phone calls.

Delilah heard a knock on the door and looked up. Her father was standing right there. "Dad?" She was shocked for a moment. "I thought you wouldn't be able to make it."

He waved her off. "It's your graduation, sweetie. I wouldn't miss this for the world."

Delilah got up and hugged her father. She felt guilty for how their last conversation went down. It felt like a lifetime ago, but she still had it close to her chest. "I'm sorry for the things I said to you."

He kissed her on the forehead. "It actually got me thinking about a lot of things." He grabbed her hand and towed her to the bed. "How are you doing?" he asked.

Delilah looked at her father. She knew he had never been around much, but she could count on him when she needed him in dire moments. She knew that he had a hectic schedule lately, and it was why she felt so much resentment toward him. She had a lot of anger ready to be poured out because of everyone. "I thought I could trust people. I felt betrayed by everyone. Mom was judging me, you weren't around, and Danielle exposed the darkest part of me to the world."

Matt knew he messed up when he wasn't there for his daughter. He should have been home to discipline her after the principal scandal came out. Matt, you shouldn't beat yourself up too much. She was given a stern talking to and a dick in the mouth by her true "father figure."

"I'm sorry for not being around as much as I should have. I assumed you were all grown up, and you didn't need me anymore. I believed you could make it on your own. You're a writer, and I thought you needed alone time to figure it out on your own."

"But I'm your daughter and I was crying out for help. I felt betrayed, abandoned, and afraid. I was starting to lose myself, and I don't know if I like who I've become." Delilah liked playing in the world of bitch, but she didn't feel satisfied anymore. She read the reviews for her short story, and she wanted to go back to that girl. She wanted to be someone that wanted to inspire the world, not destroy it.

"You're allowed to fall off the wagon sometimes. It's okay to be cruel and hurtful, but what do you have left when all of your rage is out of your system?"

She looked at him. "And that's the problem. I don't write anymore. I've been so focused on being angry that I stopped writing." She knew after today she would have her final words with Danielle. She would stab Danielle the way she stabbed her, and her anger would be gone.

He reached over and squeezed. "That makes one of my gifts to you so perfect."

She looked at him. "What do you mean?" she asked.

"I'm going on an Asian, European, and Australian book tour. It will take all summer," he said.

Danielle wanted to cry again. She thought her dad was finally getting what she was trying to say. She wanted him to be home more often. She was going off to college in the fall, and she wanted to spend time with him before she left. Our question was who accepted you into their college? You might have had

Zachary Ryan

the contest fooled, but a whole university too? Maybe you were cut out for writing, you created one hell of a story for yourself.

"When do you leave?" she asked, with a gloomy tone in her voice.

Matt could tell that his daughter looked defeated. He chuckled. "I don't think you're getting the point." Matt, you had to spell it out for her. She had the brain of a two-year-old and a mouth of a gay guy at a glory hole.

"Which is?"

"I want you to come with me on the tour. I know one day you'll have your own book tour, and this will be good practice. Plus, I want you to have this time to travel, get inspired, and write again," Matt said.

Delilah wanted nothing more than to do that. "Yes," she said, while hugging him. She squeezed tightly because she felt like it was a dream. She was getting out of New York City, and she would be with her dad. We were disappointed, because what was going to happen to Richard? We would never know.

He laughed and stood up. "I better get ready before we leave. I'm so proud of everything you've accomplished." He winked and walked out of the room.

Delilah felt like everything was falling into place. She was finally spending time with her dad, and she would be able to write with him. She was getting her life back on track, but the only problem was the text she just received from Jordan. She looked at the text. "I have all the dirt for the ceremony. This was going to be one hell of a graduation. I can't wait to see their faces."

Delilah looked at the message, and she was curious if she wanted to have her legacy be this for the rest of her life. She was about to get sweet justice on Danielle, but she didn't know if it was worth it. Delilah, this was why we hated you. You always second guessed everything. Couldn't you be heartless and worry about it later? Why not leave this town with a bang? You acted like people were going to remember your annoying, whiney ass once you left.

Chapter 42

"I feel like I should tell you, but you're going to judge me," Calvin said, pacing back and forth in his room. Danielle was currently playing with her hair. She decided she wanted to get ready at Calvin's house. Her mom would meet her at the graduation ceremony. They weren't on speaking terms, and Danielle didn't know how else to talk to her. Danielle, you didn't want to tell her how you woke up naked in bed with another guy? She would be understanding about it, right?

Calvin wanted to tell Danielle about him sleeping with Aman. It was huge news. Calvin, no one cared that you banged Aman. What we really wanted to know was how were your results.

Danielle was about to open her mouth, when she heard her phone go off. It was an unknown caller. She was hesitant to pick it up, but it could be a new client for her to seduce. "Hello?"

"Is this Ms. Danielle Tyler?"

"This is she." Danielle was curious who this would be.

"Yes, my name is Blake Rogers. I'm the assistant creative director for Fashion Weekly. You put in an application a couple months ago with us for the summer internship. We would like to congratulate you on the opportunity and wondered if you would accept the internship."

Danielle's mouth dropped. She had applied for the internship back at the beginning of the new year. She assumed she didn't get the internship because she hadn't heard anything about it. "Of course! I accept."

Blake smiled. "Excellent. I'll send you over the information, and we look forward to seeing you in the next couple of weeks." He hung up on her.

Danielle screamed. "What's wrong?" Calvin asked.

"That was the assistant creative director for Fashion Weekly. He just offered me an internship." Danielle jumped up and down.

"Holy shit," Calvin said. He pulled Danielle in and hugged her close. "I can't believe it."

Danielle was all smiles. We were proud our favorite escort was doing more with her life than staying on her back. We did wonder if her old life wouldn't be plastered all over the pages of her new magazine. Here was to hoping her secrets went viral outside of New York City.

Danielle looked at Calvin. "What did you want to tell me?" she asked.

Calvin smiled. He looked Danielle. "I can't believe we're graduating. It seems like we would never make it to this day."

Danielle knew there was something else he wanted to talk about, but she wasn't going to pry on it. She smiled gently. She pulled him into a hug. "You've always been my best friend, and I can't thank you enough for having my back."

"You know I would never give Delilah any dirt on you."

Danielle waved him off. "Because you're a true friend." Danielle paused. "Besides, she has a right to expose my dirty secrets. It's only the right thing to do."

"Do you think you two will ever be okay?" Calvin asked.

"I don't know, but I'm not going to worry about it. We're about to go to graduation, and we can put all of this behind us. We have a bright future," Danielle smiled. She still felt the excitement coursing through her body.

Calvin looked at the excitement on her face, and he wanted that for himself. This wasn't something to look forward to, and he was disappointed that he had no career ambitions anymore. Calvin, you could swap with Danielle. We heard there was a gay section on that fetish website, why didn't you give that a try?

He felt his phone go off, and he saw that it was the clinic calling. "I better get this."

"Who is it?" Danielle asked. "Is it a mystery lover?"

Calvin rolled his eyes. "You're so annoying." He walked into the hallway and answered. "Hello?"

"Is this Calvin Chase?"

"Yes, this is he."

"This is Meredith at the Smith's free clinic. You came in earlier this week for testing. We have your results back, and we need to do some follow up testing."

"Is there something wrong?" he asked.

"It could be nothing, but there was a couple of positives," she said.

Calvin, Calvin, Calvin. You had truly hit rock bottom. It looked like your nights in a park, night club bathrooms, and in gym shower were finally catching up to you. We hoped you could tell your best friend all about your fun, or would you run to Jordan with this bomb shell of news?

"Is any of it life threatening?"

"We don't want you to worry too much. It could be false positives. There is always a chance for that. We just need you to come in at your earliest convenience to get tested again."

"Okay." Calvin set up an appointment to have follow up testing done. He walked back into his room to see Danielle looked at a magazine. She had her life together, and his was a mess. We wouldn't call her life fully together, Calvin. She didn't tell you how she was being blackmailed. Both of your lives were complete trash, but she had a bit of hope to get her through it, did you?

He saw a text from Aman texting him that he couldn't wait to see him at graduation. Calvin ignored the text and went over to sit next to Danielle. They talked about Fashion Weekly, and how she couldn't wait to start her internship. These two always had a calming moment before the bomb was dropped. You should savor this moment as long as you could. You might have thought your graduation was going to be a cliché one, but we were proud to say it was nothing such.

****

Bethany was in her cap and gown reading her speech over and over. She was trying to make sure that everything sounded perfect. Bethany, we didn't get why you were trying so hard. It wasn't like people were going to listen to you. They enjoyed you as The Marked Queen, but the novelty wore off. Didn't you remember your failure of a party?

Linda walked in to see her daughter standing there. "I can't believe the day has finally come."

Bethany was mid-speech when her mother walked in. She turned to her. "Mom, this isn't the best time to have one of your special moments."

Linda chuckled. "You have nothing to worry about. Your speech is going to be perfect. Besides, you could look at me or even Tucker." She paused for a moment. "I'm surprised he didn't come over to take pictures before we got to the arena."

"Mom." Bethany knew she had to tell her mother the truth, and she wasn't looking forward to it. We could retell the story how her boyfriend dumped you for the crazy bitch currently on heroin. "Tucker and I broke up."

"What? When?" Linda looked at her.

Bethany shrugged her off. "I don't want to talk about it. I just want to focus on this speech."

Linda took a seat on Bethany's bed. "When I went through a breakup, my girlfriends were there for me. They would take me to all these house parties, and I would shamelessly flirt with boys."

Bethany had enough of her mother's stories. "Mom, we get it. You had a blast in high school and college. You had all the best friends in the world. You don't need to remind me that I have no one in my life. I don't need you to tell me that I'm some fucking loser." Bethany looked at her mother. Bethany, these were the tears we wanted you to keep for later.

Linda could tell that her daughter was upset. "Beth."

Bethany shook her head. "I need to get this speech down. Can you please leave me alone?"

Linda shook her head. "No, I won't. What do you mean, you have no one?"

Bethany knew her mother wasn't going to let it go. Were you going to tell her the whole truth or make you be the victim? "Mom, I've always been the wallflower. I've never been the popular girl like you were."

"I know that, but you have no friends? What about that Susan girl?"

Bethany rolled her eyes. "She wasn't someone you could call loyal." Bethany was also jealous of Susan. She was able to make friends so easily. She wished she had that ability.

Bethany, she was also crazy. You were a bitch, but at least you didn't have mental breakdowns caught on camera.

Linda pulled her daughter into a hug. She was disappointed that Bethany was never fully honest with her. She didn't care if she wasn't the most popular girl, but she wanted to have memories she could have for the rest of her life. Linda, you should be upset you raised a rejected bitch. We would be in tears if we were you.

"Bethany, I'm so proud of you. I want you to never forget that. Your father is watching you from above, and he would be smiling." Linda looked in her daughter's eyes. "You've always been focused, strong, and adventurous. Those are qualities I wish I had in someone. I never could survive on my own, and I'm so thankful you got that from your father. I needed everyone to get me through life, and you said hell with all of it. I want you to go into today proud of all the accomplishments you've achieved."

Bethany smiled and embraced the kiss her mother gave her on the forehead. "Thank you." Bethany needed that before she gave her speech later. She took in a deep breath. "I'm glad we had this emotional moment, but I really need to get this speech down."

"I can't wait to hear it." She walked toward the door. "You might believe you're the wall flower, but they will remember you today. All eyes are going to be on you. You should relish your moment in the spotlight." She walked out of the room, leaving Bethany with those thoughts.

Bethany, we wanted you to take your mother's words very seriously. You were about to be in front of all your graduating class. You were going to have your moment in the spotlight again. The only difference was, you were the prey this time. You

Zachary Ryan

stood proud after prom, but you wouldn't be smiling or toasting once The Revenged Queen was done with you. Hoped you brought tissues and a new identity. You were going to need it.

Chapter 43

Graduation is a time of self-reflect and self-appreciation. It was a moment in a person's life where they felt accomplished. The students of Johnson Prep had been chained to a prison for eighteen-years, and they were finally being released. People came together to give students their congrats. A Johnson Prep graduation was a bit different. There would be tears of course, some laughter, and as always, a little drama. It might have been a small, intimate moment between a hundred students, but the stories from this ceremony would be told to millions.

Danielle and Calvin walked into the banquet hall where the graduation ceremony would take place. There was time before the ceremony began, and the students were supposed to wait it out. Danielle saw that she had a missed call from her father. She hadn't talked to him in weeks, and she wondered why he was calling. She looked at Calvin. "Are you going to be okay for a second?" she asked.

He turned to her. He was still in a haze thinking about his test results. He wanted to believe that it was a false positive. "What?"

Danielle looked at him. "Are you okay?"

He smiled. "Yeah, I guess it's all hitting me that we're graduating."

She kissed him on the cheek. "We still have summer before we say our final goodbyes." She winked and walked away to try to call her father. She didn't know that she would get ahold of him, but you would eventually find out what his phone call was for. You had better prepare yourself Danielle because you were in for one hell of a summer.

Zachary Ryan

Aman walked up to Calvin. Aman felt a weight lifted off his shoulder. "Calvin, hey."

Calvin turned to see Aman. Calvin's insides started to twist and turn. He thought he might throw up. The one person he didn't want to see right then was Aman. He didn't regret them hooking up, but he didn't want to go back into that cage as much as he wished he didn't get out of it. He might have been filled with sin, but he was able to be proud of who he was. "Aman, it's good to see you."

"Can we talk?" Aman asked.

Calvin nodded. "Sure."

Aman escorted him to two of the seats. "So, I wanted to talk to you real quick."

"About?" Calvin asked.

"Us," Aman said. "I know that it hasn't been easy the past couple of months with us." Aman paused to really appreciate Calvin's beauty. He was really missing this, and he wanted them to work out. "I'm ready to come out to my parents."

Aman, you were full of surprises. We never thought you would grow the balls to come out. We would like to commend you, but we hoped you had better luck than Calvin. Although, we were curious what places you would do your dirty deeds, and it had better not be with Calvin. We didn't want romance, we wanted slutty mistakes.

"Is this because of what happened in the dugout?" Calvin asked. He was over the moon that Aman was ready to come out. He had been wanting this for months. "I don't want you to feel like you have to come out because of me."

Aman shook his head. "No, I'm ready to come out. I'm tired of having to live a double life. If my family disowns me for being gay, then that's something I have to accept." Aman squeezed his hand. "I really want us to work out, Calvin. I've missed you too much, and I've never stopped loving you. I pray we can make it work."

"I love you, too," Calvin replied. He felt the high of this excitement for a quick second, until the reality set it. You needed to tell him about your little doctor's appointment in the next couple of days. We hoped and prayed he would be understanding of the actual reality going on. Aman was still in love with you, and you were too busy getting your hole filled by every thirsty top in the city.

Calvin didn't get a chance to respond, before they were told to get in positions for the ceremony. We won't bore you with the useless information about the ceremony — if you had been to a graduation ceremony, you know the students come in, people make speeches, and it gets very boring.

Bethany and Delilah were in the room where all the students were being held. They were both about to walk in to give their own speeches. Bethany would go first to give the valedictorian speech, then Delilah would read her short story that she won the contest with.

Bethany was introduced. The doors opened, and Bethany walked down the aisle with the graduating class on both sides of her toward the stage. The doors closed, and Delilah was left alone. She felt like a ball of nerves. Why were you so nervous Delilah? We knew it wasn't because of your short story. Did it have to do with you about to expose Danielle's secret to the whole school? Were you feeling guilty for it?

The door opened, and Delilah saw Jordan walking in. "Did she just go in?" Jordan asked.

"Yes."

Jordan smiled. "Perfect. It's about to be showtime."

"Maybe we shouldn't do this," Delilah said. Delilah realized that she didn't want to do this anymore. She knew she still felt hurt from what Danielle did, but she was worse than what Danielle did.

Jordan ignored her. "You can keep your guilty conscious for your diary. I'm here to ruin a bitch's life." Jordan flung the doors open. The graduating class turned to see Jordan making her entrance. Bethany stopped mid-speech, and all eyes were on the intruder.

Jordan walked down the aisle. She looked straight at The Marked Queen. She had to admit she looked kind of frumpy in her cap and gown. She might have thought her big moment was happening right now, but The Revenged Queen was here to steal it from her. She was dressed in a black dress looking like the black widow herself. Too bad for the ones caught in Jordan's web, they weren't going to survive the ambush. "What are you doing?" Bethany asked.

Jordan smirked. "Just taking a page from your book." She pulled out her phone and pressed send before dropping the useless phone on the ground. The mass text message contained Danielle's link to her fetish website, a video of Susan's meltdown during her high school play, Bethany's real grades, and the medical document for her abortion. "Enjoy the rest of your graduation ceremony, I know you're never going to forget the day you went from being valedictorian to being an embarrassment of this school." Jordan turned and walked away letting her venomous bite slowly eat Bethany alive.

****

People stood there in silence for a moment, before the whole room went into a chaos frenzy. People started looking at the links of Danielle in her skimpiest outfits. Danielle, completely mortified, saw her mother's disappointed facial expressions. Susan had a complete meltdown after people started laughing from watching her video. She screamed and ran out of the building to get away from the stares.

Bethany wasn't so lucky. She had to stand in front of everyone as people found out her true dirt. She saw the stares and whispers. She stood there motionless, trying to keep herself become composed. She wanted to fall to the ground in that instant. She turned to see her mother looking at her with worry.

Bethany wasn't going to let some bitch take her moment away from her. "Class of 2018," she screamed into the crowd. Everyone looked forward and was silent. "Let us ignore that interruption and get back to my speech."

Eddie screamed whore because he was a classless pig. He had the wealth of a billionaire and the poise of a trailer park white trash, wife beater. People laughed, but Bethany ignored them. She continued with her speech until she was finished. No one clapped for her speech, and Bethany wasn't surprised.

Delilah was introduced next. She read her short story without looking at Danielle. Why wouldn't you look at the person you just humiliated? It wasn't like you just ruined her life? Delilah ran off the stage as quickly as possible. There was one last speech, the high school diplomas, and everyone was released. They were thrilled to leave that room, because damn did they have gossip to spread. We told you a Johnson Prep ceremony would not be like the other ceremonies you had been to.

Delilah quickly went up to Danielle. "I'm so sorry for what I did. I didn't mean to expose you like that," Delilah said.

Danielle put a finger in the air. She wanted to be pissed with Delilah, but she couldn't. She knew she deserved this, and it felt nice to have her secrets exposed to the world again. She also knew that Christian couldn't use this against her anymore. The world knew what she did for money, and she couldn't care less. "Delilah, you were getting your revenge out after what I did to you. I'm just going to chalk it up to karma."

Delilah was expecting Danielle to be furious. "So… you're not mad?"

Danielle just graduated. She had an internship to look forward to. If someone gave a shit about their dark past, it wasn't her. Danielle, when would you learn the true lesson in all of this? You might have been done with your past, but your past wasn't done with you yet, bitch. "Yeah, I don't care. I'm over this drama, and I have a fashion internship to focus on."

Delilah smiled. "I'm actually leaving for the summer. My dad asked me to go on a book tour with him."

Danielle knew how much Delilah wanted time with her father, and she was happy she was getting out of New York to do it. "It's good to hear that."

"I'll see you around. Maybe we can patch things up when I get back."

"I would like that," Danielle said. That was a boring fight. We wanted you two to have another cat fight. We had to have some kind of resolution in this story, didn't we? We hoped they learned their lesson and didn't do it again.

Delilah found her parents. "Let's get out of here," she said. Delilah turned to her classmates that she had grown up with. She sighed and smiled. She might have some dark moments in her years with them, but she felt like she found her strength from it. Delilah, we hoped you inspired the world like you promised, but we hoped you told a scandalous story or two along the way. We wished you the best, and we hoped you kept your bitchy side for anytime the publishing world became too ruthless.

"I think I owe you an apology," Lily said, walking up to her daughter.

Danielle turned to her mother. She was tired of apologies. "Mom, I don't want to have another sentimental day. I just want to go home. I know you were trying to protect me. I forgive you."

Lily was pleased to see her daughter didn't hold too much anger inside her chest toward her. She pulled her daughter in for a hug. "Thank you."

"No problem." Danielle didn't realize how much she needed this hug. She wanted her and her mother to be back on better terms. She knew they would have their bumps, but she hoped now that she had graduated and was an adult they could work on a more civil relationship. Danielle, did you really think that was going to happen? You had better get ready because now that you grew up, the real fun could begin.

People started exiting and Calvin came up to Danielle. "I didn't know you were so limber," he said.

Danielle saw he was watching one of her videos. She grabbed the phone out of his hand and smacked him upside the head. "You're such an asshole."

He laughed. "Now you're no longer the poor girl."

"Least that's a positive."

"Hey, it could be worse. People are talking about Susan's meltdown today in that video, and they're going crazy over Bethany's abortion."

"Why can't one thing in our life be ordinary?" Danielle asked, thinking about prom and now graduation.

Calvin shrugged. "It's Johnson Prep. We don't really do traditional."

"Do you know where Bethany went?" Danielle asked.

"What I heard was, she went out the side entrance quietly. Her mom was waiting with the car, so she didn't have to see her new fans."

Danielle laughed. "I guess there goes her rise to the top."

Calvin put his arm around Danielle's shoulder. "We survived another truth bomb together."

Danielle looked at Calvin. "I guess that's a positive in all of this." They laughed and walked out of the building together. No matter what happened, they still had their friendship intact. They were going to need their friendship because this summer was going to be one bitch of an ending for our favorite students of Johnson Prep. Hoped they wore enough sunblock and condoms, and kept the knives sharpen for a classic backstabbing.

****

Jordan got into her limo with such pride. She told the driver to take her home. She basked in the reality that she had taken her spot on the throne. Jordan, we were thrilled you were the queen bee of Johnson Prep class of 2019. We hoped you didn't make a mistake like Danielle. We didn't want the wallflowers to take over again.

Jordan was looking at the comments and texts from her little show during the graduation ceremony. It all happened so quickly that she didn't know how to process what was happening. One moment she was sitting and enjoying herself, then she was being thrown across her limo.

Jordan tried to get up, but the pain was too unbearable. She tried to scream for help, but she was too weak. She could hear people scream around her and the sound of a car alarm. It took a moment for Jordan to realize she had been in a car accident. The day that was supposed to be her brightest moment, had turned into a tragedy.

She didn't want to go out this way. She had better survive. She tried to reach for her phone. She needed to call Alassane. She knew no one else would come to her rescue. She felt the tears fall down her face. She gathered all her strength to grab her phone and pulled it close to her. She opened her text messages.

Jordan slowly felt the darkness take over. She knew she wouldn't have enough time to text Alassane. She closed her eyes because she didn't want to admit that she was going to leave this world the way she lived it, alone.

She heard her phone go off. She looked to see it was a text from an anonymous number. She clicked on the message.

Unknown Number: *You just took your seat at the top. Too bad for you, now you have enemies coming for your throne. I watched you and the rest of these bitches hurt and destroy each other. It's time that someone puts a stop to it. No one deserves to be terrorized by any of you anymore. Sleep tight knowing one of the dragons in this kingdom has been slain.*

Jordan felt a surge of adrenaline. She wasn't going to let this random bitch win. She wanted to process the fact that someone had tried to murder her, but she wasn't going to let her killer get the satisfaction. She used all her strength to call 911.

The operator asked Jordan what her emergency was, but Jordan didn't get the chance to respond. We weren't expecting an actual blood bath, but we didn't mind some carnage. It looked like another queen was coming for the crown, but she had a different tactic. The only question we had on our mind was who was this new villain, and what horrors she had up her sleeve? We watched Jordan cry and take her last breath, and we had one thing left to say to her, "Bye, bitch."

About the Publisher

#KINGSTONPUBLISHING

www.kingstonpublishing.com

Kingston Publishing offers an affordable way for you to turn your dream into a reality. We offer every service you will ever need to take an idea and publish a story. We are here to help authors make it in the industry. We've been hurt by publishers in the past and we want to provide a positive experience that will keep you coming back to us.

Whether you want a traditional publisher who offers all the amenities a publishing company should or an author who prefers to self-publish, but needs additional help - we are here for you.

Now Accepting Manuscripts!

Please send query letter and manuscript to:

submissions@kingstonpublishing.com

Visit our website at www.kingstonpublishing.com

CPSIA information can be obtained
at www.ICGtesting.com
Printed in the USA
LVHW022335120619
621079LV00007B/123/P

9 781645 331339